SECOND CHANCE SEAL

Sunset SEALs Book 2

SHARON HAMILTON

SHARON HAMILTON'S BOOK LIST

SEAL BROTHERHOOD BOOKS

SEAL BROTHERHOOD SERIES
Accidental SEAL Book 1
Fallen SEAL Legacy Book 2
SEAL Under Covers Book 3
SEAL The Deal Book 4
Cruisin' For A SEAL Book 5
SEAL My Destiny Book 6
SEAL of My Heart Book 7
Fredo's Dream Book 8
SEAL My Love Book 9
SEAL Encounter Prequel to Book 1
SEAL Endeavor Prequel to Book 2
Ultimate SEAL Collection Vol. 1 Books 1-4 /2 Prequels
Ultimate SEAL Collection Vol. 2 Books 5-7

SEAL BROTHERHOOD LEGACY SERIES
Watery Grave Book 1
Honor The Fallen Book 2
Grave Injustice Book 3
Deal With The Devil Book 4

BAD BOYS OF SEAL TEAM 3 SERIES
SEAL's Promise Book 1
SEAL My Home Book 2
SEAL's Code Book 3
Big Bad Boys Bundle Books 1-3

Sunset SEALs Duet #2

LOVE VIXEN
Bone Frog Love

SHADOW SEALS
Shadow of the Heart
Shadow Warrior

SILVER SEALS SERIES
SEAL Love's Legacy

SLEEPER SEALS SERIES
Bachelor SEAL

STAND ALONE BOOKS & SERIES
SEAL's Goal: The Beautiful Game
Nashville SEAL: Jameson
True Blue SEALS Zak
Paradise: In Search of Love
Love Me Tender, Love You Hard

NOVELLAS
SEAL You In My Dreams Magnolias and Moonshine

PARANORMALS

GOLDEN VAMPIRES OF TUSCANY SERIES
Honeymoon Bite Book 1
Mortal Bite Book 2
Christmas Bite Book 3
Midnight Bite Book 4

THE GUARDIANS
Heavenly Lover Book 1
Underworld Lover Book 2
Underworld Queen Book 3
Redemption Book 4

FALL FROM GRACE SERIES
Gideon: Heavenly Fall

NOVELLAS
SEAL Of Time Trident Legacy

All of Sharon's books are available on Audible,
narrated by the talented J.D. Hart.

ABOUT THE BOOK

Navy SEAL Damon Hamblin's life is in turmoil after he's served with divorce papers during his last deployment. He crashes into a sleepy Florida Gulf Coast town to drown his sorrows and just fade into the background, where no one knows him and he can drink, surf and lay out on the beach until his insides heal. The last thing he wants is to rebound into another relationship.

Martel Long came to Sunset Beach five years ago to visit a friend, and never left. She's tried to forget the man who broke her heart back home, and had been doing a good job of it, until she comes face to face with him at a Bachelorette party for her best friend at a local beach bar.

As sparks fly and old wounds are torn open, the sands at Sunset Beach help to heal a beautiful love story that could have been, and will be again.

AUTHOR'S NOTE

I always dedicate my SEAL Brotherhood books to the brave men and women who defend our shores and keep us safe. Without their sacrifice, and that of their families—because a warrior's fight always includes his or her family—I wouldn't have the freedom and opportunity to make a living writing these stories. They sometimes pay the ultimate price so we can debate, argue, go have coffee with friends, raise our children and see them have children of their own.

One of my favorite tributes to warriors resides on many memorials, including one I saw honoring the fallen of WWII on an island in the Pacific:

> "When you go home
> Tell them of us, and say
> For your tomorrow,
> We gave our today."

These are my stories created out of my own imagination. Anything that is inaccurately portrayed is either my mistake, or done intentionally to disguise something I might have overheard over a beer or in the corner of one of the hangouts along the Coronado Strand.

I support two main charities. Navy SEAL/UDT Museum operates in Ft. Pierce, Florida. Please learn about this wonderful museum, all run by active and former SEALs and their friends and families, and who rely on public support, not that of the U.S. Government. www.navysealmuseum.org

IF YOU GOT ANY CLOSER, YOU WOULD HAVE TO ENLIST

I also support Wounded Warriors, who tirelessly bring together the warrior as well as the family members who are just learning to deal with their soldier's condition and have nowhere to turn. It is a long path to becoming well, but I've seen first-hand what this organization does for its warriors and the families who love them. Please give what your heart tells you is right. If you cannot give, volunteer at one of the many service centers all over the United States. Get involved. Do something meaningful for someone who gave so much of themselves, to families who have paid the price for your freedom. You'll find a family there unlike any other on the planet.

www.woundedwarriorproject.org

CHAPTER 1

"**N**OW THIS IS what I'm talking about!" He poked his head outside, through the ten-inch opening in the sliding glass door and breathed in the cool early morning air.

Bright blue sky. Shockingly white sugar sand beach. Not a cloud anywhere. Waves lapping on the shore. Nobody there.

Special Operator Damon Hamlin of SEAL Team 3 knew this place would heal the black tarry puddle that was his soul.

"A few beers, some margaritas, some moonlight sex, some wasted days. That oughta do it. Maybe I won't go back," he whispered to himself.

A month ago, his soon-to-be-ex-wife, Charlene, had sent those papers straight to the forward camp they were holding up in Benin, West Africa. Of course, she didn't care that he was putting his life on the line, trying to find bad guys. She just wanted out.

I knew it was a mistake to leave after we had that big fight.

But he never thought she would actually go to the trouble of actually attempting to have their marriage dissolved without as much as a phone call first. No, the woman couldn't wait to shed off his carcass like a snake sheds his skin. More than likely, it was because she'd found herself another guy to perform unspeakable things to her body. That was Charlene, doing everything to excess. He'd liked it at first. Considered her a challenge. In the end, it was just drama, nothing but drama.

In the thick manila envelope was a cover letter by her female attorney. Very terse and efficient, the letter spelled out the instructions for ending what was a volatile marriage anyway. There wasn't an ounce of compassion or warmth in the words. And Charlene's only personal part in all the papers was that she signed it. A "wet" signature, they called it. That was all she could muster. Probably all that was required.

Wives who did this to active duty SEALs overseas on assignment were especially disliked on the Teams, and when word got round that Charlene had chosen to make their dissolution so public, he had got a lot of support. And that pissed him off too. Damon was *not* a wounded warrior. He had all his parts, even if he had a hole the size of California in his heart.

His BUD/S and nearly ten-year buddy from Team 3, Renny Walker, had slept in the bunk beneath him in their railroad car bunker home-away-from-home—the closest thing he'd ever gotten to an African safari.

"I've got to go to Florida to be at this wedding. When we get back home, why don't you tag along with me?" Renny had teased, his hairy blond legs protruding from below.

That got Damon thinking. What else did he have to live for? His job after he got home was always to get whole. That meant making sure he created some vivid memories that would wipe out any past Charlene history. Those were legendary fights and incredible make-up sex. He'd have to stuff all those things down just in case he was tempted to go soft and try to win her back. He didn't consider that to be a manly thing at all.

"I'm game. But I have no idea where to stay or…I've never been to Florida before. Don't they have crocs and hurricanes and shit like that, Renny?"

"Crocs are damned good eating when you can get them, and we haven't had a hurricane at that part of the coast in over fifty years. But don't stress about a thing. We've rented five little bungalows all next to each other on the beach. You can stay with me. They're not huge but do have a bedroom and a decent-sized living room with a memory foam couch that is supposed to be comfortable. And, Demon Seed, it's right on the beach, in case I didn't say it before. *On the beach!*"

Renny had been right. This view, the smell of the water, the sounds of the wind and sea birds as well as the waves lapping on the shore was exactly what he needed. It would save him from having to drink several gallons of alcohol on his road to oblivion. His liver and kidneys would be thankful.

It was freakin' gorgeous here. He liked staring at the horizon, that place where the sky and the blue water mated. Uncomplicated. It didn't require any fuzzy logic, or any logic at all. It was an answer to prayer he hadn't had the courage to ask.

They'd gotten in so late last night that all he had seen were the stars in the sky and moonlight twinkling on the water. But he heard the waves all night long as he slept with the slider open.

Yup, Renny's descriptions of Sunset Beach were totally accurate.

He stepped into his trunks, slid on his flip-flops, pulled a T-shirt up from the tiled floor by the hide-a-bed where he'd tossed it last night, and made his way out, over the sand dunes and onto the white sugary beach. The glare and brightness gave him a headache, and he resolved to get a decent pair of sunglasses ASAP.

Black dots formed to the right and the left of him at the shoreline, which later morphed into people going or coming towards him. He let the early morning moisture kiss his face clean, which settled the headache he'd developed from all the drinks he and Renny imbibed on the plane ride from California.

Damon turned right for no good reason and marched over the white sand littered with ocean debris. Broken pieces of shells, water-worn twigs, and pieces of sea glass, and rocks crunched under the weight of his flip-flops as he walked. Two elderly gentlemen on fat tire motorized bicycles zoomed past him from behind.

"Morning, pilgrim," the one with the ponytail called out, his voice booming in a deep Southern drawl.

"Nice ride!" he answered back, admiring the expensive bikes. Their electric motors quietly did the work their legs didn't have to, and it made him want to get one for himself. The tires reminded him of the old Schwinn he had when he was a kid, even though his dad had bought him a girl's bike. The beast was way bigger than his little legs could pedal and stay seated. However, it saved injury to his balls, even though his classmates gave him all kinds of hell at school.

But they were wheels, and allowed him increased autonomy and mobility.

And a little trouble occasionally.

He heard his name called so he turned to see Renny

standing in the backyard with a bright beach towel slung low around his waist.

"Hey, asshole, we're going out for breakfast with the groom and guys from the wedding party. Are you coming?" Renny shouted at him.

Damon's stomach was in dire need of something to settle it down. "Don't mind if I do," he answered. He attempted to run up the beach in his flip-flops but nearly tripped, so he removed them and ran barefoot the rest of the way.

The girl Renny had picked up last night stood behind him, also wrapped in a towel. She looked a lot younger this morning than she did in the bar last night. Her flawless tanned skin showed no evidence of her swimsuit line, either. Renny was more practiced in the art of dating since he'd been divorced for over five years. Legendary for picking real beauties, he preferred blondes. This one was stunning.

"Hi, Shannon," Damon mumbled in her direction, making her blush.

She waved back at him with three fingers on her left hand, clutching Renny's shoulder with her right.

"So you want to ride with us then?" asked Renny.

"Can I shower first?"

"Yup. The bathroom is all yours."

THE GROOM AND best man along with two other of

their friends had already seated themselves in the corner at a long table. Renny made the introductions.

"Hey, Greg, this is my Team brother—Damon—I told you about. I hope you don't mind that I asked him to tag along this morning."

The very tall groom with white-blonde hair, blue eyes, and a muscular frame, leaned across the table after he stood, gripping Damon's hand to the point of causing pain. Damon hated guys who did this. But he made sure he was able to pass a little pain back in his direction, in case Greg turned out to be a real prick.

"Welcome, Damon. Anybody who's with this asshole is a friend of mine."

They took their seats as several other members of the wedding party filed in. Soon the table was filled with platters of eggs, bacon, and pancakes the size of dinner plates. Damon stuffed himself nearly to the point of explosion. He decided this would be a fitting way to begin his days of excess.

"How do you know Greg?" he asked Renny after the other introductions were made.

"He and I worked construction one summer before I came to Coronado. He was headed to the Air Force to go for the Pararescue Swim Program until they discovered the poor bastard had a vision problem and was rejected. Can't be a pilot if you have bad eyes. We stayed in touch. I went off to BUD/S, and he got a pretty good job running a large construction crew, later owned his own business framing new homes. Somehow he wandered into a real estate office, and they talked him into sales. We were running around in our boxers, getting shot at, and killing those bugs the size of our little fingers—you remember those fuckers that smelled so bad?"

"Hard to forget those little Vienna Sausages."

"Yeah, well, he was wearing a suit and making more than Admiral Byrne times two. I think he'd already bought a home by the time we re-upped."

"Smart dude."

"Now he's marrying a rich girl. Dad was a big developer before he passed. We stayed friends, and he came out to San Diego once. Can't remember what you were doing then."

"I think I remember him. You brought him to one of the bonfires years ago right?"

"Yeah, I did. I didn't realize I shouldn't have. Kyle told me later on. He never liked Greg."

"I didn't like him either. 'Course I kind of thought he had an eye on Charlene."

"That's because Charlene had an eye on *him*. But don't feel bad. She was interested in *everybody*."

"Don't fuckin' tell me that. That's so disrespectful." It was spoiling Damon's appetite.

Renny grinned back at him, appearing not to take

the comment to heart. He wrapped his arm around Damon's shoulder. "Best thing that ever happened to you. Did you get that tattoo?"

Damon had promised to remove Charlene's initials from his left bicep and replace it with a naked lady. "Didn't have time," he mumbled. Several of the groom's party were staring at them, so he shrugged off Renny's arm. "Get off me."

"Now you're acting like a teenager. That's how all newly divorced men act."

"Except it's not official."

"Impending divorce. Excuse me, Professor Demon Seed."

"Fuck you, Renny. I seemed to remember you having trouble adjusting to your single life back in the day. I'm just out of practice, man. And for the record, if you tell another lady I'm getting divorced I'm going to take you down or pour sand in your fuckin' bed. So lay off."

Renny was wiggling his eyebrows down to the other end of the table, connecting with some of Greg's friends. "Suit yourself, but don't be so touchy," he whispered out of the side of his mouth. "It wasn't your fault at all. All on her. A character flaw."

"So I'm discovering." Damon shoveled more pancakes and chased them down with a newly refilled mug of black coffee.

Several of the guys were telling stories about a recent fishing trip on the bay.

"So all these guys are from LA then, or Florida?"

"Some from LA, a couple guys from Sacramento, and Dieter over there is from Chicago, but he's German. The guy at the end of the table is Greg's brother, Brian. You want to keep your distance from that guy when he's drunk."

"Anybody military or served?" Damon wanted to know.

"Nah, I think it's just you and me, Damon. Greg was going to try out, but he dropped, due to his eyes again."

Damon began to feel comfortable with the group. Nearly all of them appeared to be about thirty years of age, the same age as he and Renny.

Greg leaned over and spoke directly to Damon. "I'm sort of on lockdown. Last year, one of Kaitlyn's friends had a groom they sent to Alaska during his bachelor party, and he missed the wedding."

"Holy crap. We had a Team guy that happened to. Do you remember who that was, Renny?"

"Yeah. Don't remember his name. Never did get married to her, as I recall." Renny shrugged, making a face to the groom.

Greg shook his head. "Well, they had the party without the ceremony, and the bride and groom had to get married at the courthouse when he got back. But

Kaitlyn didn't want me to get any ideas."

"She sounds worried," chuckled Renny.

"Actually, it was her mother who made me promise every time I see her I won't let it happen." Greg gave a bright white grin to the two SEALs. "Like I said, I'm on lockdown. I love her, so I get to put up with this. I'm under strict orders. No strippers, no pole dancers, no naked orgies, and I have to come home on my own two feet, not carried."

"Shaken but not stirred," whistled Renny.

"Exactly."

Damon decided to mess with him a little bit. "So trannys and hookers are okay then?"

Greg and most of his party erupted in laughter. He mimicked using a firearm. "Bingo." And then he added, "He's all right, Renny. You hangin' out with us tonight? I like the way your mind works."

"Up to the kid here." Renny pointed his thumb at Damon.

"Sounds like fun. I got a few demons to exorcise. I might need some help with that," answered Damon.

"So I heard."

"Dammit, Renny. Who *haven't* you told?" he spat back to his buddy.

"That's it, sport. My lips will be sealed from now on," said Renny.

"Then it's settled." Greg gave him a high-five.

"Warning, Kaitlyn and some of her girlfriends are pretty distracting. I'd say it's a good bet you'll find what you're looking for. And, if not, it will find you, for sure!"

DAMON WAS GLAD he'd packed one nice Aloha shirt and a long pair of jeans, even though it was warm. He wore his flip-flops. Renny drove them to the Crab Shack, which had a huge wraparound outdoor bar. Twinkle light-encrusted umbrellas decorated the tables. Instead of sawdust on the floor, like some of the haunts in San Diego, the patio was covered in crushed bleached white shells. He was getting used to the sound of the crunching beneath his feet.

A small band played island tunes. In the corner, several kids played horseshoes and darts. Renny cruised by the outside bar, picked up two long-necked beers made at a microbrewery in Florida, handed one to Damon, and sauntered across the patio to a large group of men and ladies. Damon recognized Greg right away. Renny discovered Shannon sitting with a couple of her girlfriends. She greeted him warmly.

Damon pulled on his beer and scanned the room. A few older couples hung to the outsides of the patio, but the center section was packed with men and women in their twenties and thirties. Some were dancing. Some, like in the group with Greg, were seated on picnic tables and stools, while some were eating dinner. The music was light and happy. The band had a steel drum, and the singer's tenor voice was fresh and upbeat. The heat of the day was wearing off, beginning to turn nippy. He abandoned Renny, who was preoccupied with Shannon anyway.

He stood at the fringes of a circle of men he recognized from his breakfast and tried to listen to their banter but found he couldn't hear. When the band stopped, he finally caught a few words. They were talking about going fishing and football, just as Renny had told him they would.

He noticed how pale his arms were in comparison to the other men he stood next to. He was going to have to fix that as soon as he could.

A group of four ladies made their way over toward Greg and the other men.

Damon felt like a teenager. Renny was right. He'd been married to Charlene for nearly four years, so he did feel rusty just going up to a lady and talking to her. Examining his hands, he noticed, to his horror, he'd left his wedding ring on, so he slipped it off and stored it in his front jeans pocket.

He was examining how the pale spot on his 4th finger was such a telltale sign, just as Greg put his arm around him and began introducing him to the four new ladies. Each one was more beautiful than the previous one. Greg tried to get the attention of the fourth lady, who was watching Renny and Shannon. When she turned at Greg's instruction, he recognized her immediately.

His mouth became parched, his tongue nearly stuck to the roof. He worked on his composure. When their eyes met, her smile and the twinkle in her eyes instantly vanished.

"And this little lady is Martel. She's one of my bride's best friends and a real Florida gal now, but she comes from Northern California too."

Damon couldn't move.

"I'm not sure she's ever met a genuine Navy SEAL, Damon. I was hoping you'd make her first time memorable," Greg whispered.

Martel began a step backward and looked to the floor.

"Whoa! Hold on there, little lady. He doesn't bite," the groom said. "Damon, say hello to Martel."

He knew exactly how her hand would feel as he shook it tentatively, which made him curse himself. He firmed up his handshake and vowed to act like an adult, for Chrissakes.

She'd filled out nicely in the nearly ten years since they'd last seen each other. Her dark hair hung long over her shoulders, even though he tried not to gawk. He knew she had a diamond stud in her belly button because he'd kissed that darned thing dozens of times. He inhaled, which was another stupid idea. Her familiar scent filled him with all the memories of their fledgling romance when she was so new to sex. After all these years, he still felt the guilt of taking her virginity from her just before he ran away to his enlistment. It was something he was forever ashamed of. He'd used her. And he'd never forget the look on her face when he did it.

Ever since, he'd tried to brush it aside and couldn't. It wasn't just the guilt, but something else he couldn't put his finger on. Something dangerous, just like those reminders of how he'd awakened her with soft kisses to her abdomen. And, he'd wondered just about every day whatever had happened to her. In his string of romances and one-night stands, she was the one girl, if he ever saw her again, he wanted to apologize to. It didn't age well, either. His thirty-year-old self now understood the depth of the violation he'd caused to this gentle soul who'd been so avid to please him. He'd been too dumb and stupid to understand it at the time.

She looked like an angel. Maybe not quite as wholesome as she did when she was not-yet-twenty, but an angel all the same.

She glanced up at him briefly and then lowered her eyes again, examining her toes.

Greg had been watching the two of them and their

strange interaction. Damon knew the groom had a sharp radar. He wasn't helpful. "Damon here is—"

"Don't. Just don't, will you?" he barked at Greg, his voice sharp, stopping the groom from blabbing about his upcoming divorce. He made a mental note to have that private conversation with his new friend, even if it got him disinvited to the wedding.

"Okay, okay. Well, I'll leave you to get acquainted then," Greg said, chuckling and shaking his head as he left in search of the bar.

She wasn't going to look at him, but the awkwardness had to be filled. He sucked it up.

"Hi, Martel. Well, this is a surprise," his voice cracked, annoying him. He was an idiot to continue to hold her hand, so he dropped it quickly.

"No kidding. A SEAL, huh?" she said as she quickly studied his face and then cast her eyes downward again. "So you made it. I always thought you would." She continued to study her pink toes. He vaguely remembered her toes used to turn him on a bunch too.

Christ! Get a grip.

"Yeah, well, some guys do dumb things. I'm a sucker for getting blown up and jumping out of airplanes. It suited me after all." He shrugged. "Who knew?"

"Makes perfect sense," she said as she let her chocolate eyes fall on his face. He noted a bit of hardness there she was trying to mask.

Of course, why wouldn't she be mad, hurt or both?

He used to get lost in her chocolate brown eyes and was leaning toward her in spite of himself.

"I—I don't know what to say, Martel." The truth was, he had a lot to say, but he didn't want to say it. Then he noticed she had broken out in a sweat, little beads of perspiration hovering in the fine hairs above her upper lip. Her ample chest, alluringly helped by some undergarment that was completely invisible, developed reddish marks he knew to be from nerves. She was shaking like the first time he'd kissed her—her first real man kiss, not like the boys she was used to. He'd never told her he had been as scared as she was when he did it.

He cursed his insides, his courage failing him. This was not at all the way he expected to react when he saw her again.

"You look the same. Older, more muscles, Damon, but the same. Your face is harder." She stumbled on her next words. "I wasn't prepared for this." She squinted as if the sound of her own voice stung her.

"Yes. What are the odds?" He knew it was stupid. Completely stupid. He shook out his hands at his sides.

"Martel—"

What was he going to tell her? Was his fucking apology going to just spring out like his dick did sometimes? All he would do was violate her all over again. He hated that thought too.

"Damon, I'm not feeling very well. It was nice seeing you again."

She was lying, but she was brave. Her hand stuck out, and he did the gentlemanly thing. He accepted the shake.

"Yes, it was nice. You look great, Martel. You really do."

He knew it sounded like a consolation prize. He just couldn't get the right words. He hadn't had enough alcohol to get loosened up.

She glared at him and turned to go, after extracting her hand forcefully.

Brian, the groom's brother, approached before she uttered her final good-byes. He grabbed her elbow and spun her around to face him. Damon didn't like the way his hands were too familiar with her.

"Martel, remember, you promised me a dance?" he said.

"Oh, thanks, but I'm not feeling well and was just leaving."

"Nonsense! I'm not taking no for an answer," Brian insisted, winking at Damon.

Damon wasn't laughing, and neither was Martel.

Before she could protest, Brian had pulled her onto the dance floor, where his arms wrapped around her tiny waist like an octopus. With fucking suction cups.

Brian drew her into his intimate space, her body pressed hard against his, as he moved her around the dance floor in full control and for his own pleasure, not hers.

All Damon was able to do was watch the two of them. Had he just missed his shot to defend her? To demonstrate he was a better man today than way back then?

He thought perhaps he had.

But no mission ever worked out exactly as they planned, something he'd learned during the years of training and the deployments to unstable parts of the world. He was more prepared now for the unexpected. He also understood he was being given the chance to right the wrong he'd done to her, if she'd let him.

She didn't look for him when the dance was completed but walked straight to the pretty lady in the hot pink dress he guessed was the bride. They hugged and kissed and then Martel slipped inside the building and was gone from sight.

He'd been lukewarm about attending the wedding. Seeing Martel again had never been part of the plan. But suddenly, he knew there wasn't anything in the world that could keep him away.

CHAPTER 2

M ARTEL CLIMBED INTO her red Fiat, but before starting the engine, she laid her forehead against the padded steering wheel.

Why? Why now?

She'd spent the past five years proving to herself that moving clear across the country to Florida was the best way to forget him. She'd finally gotten to the stage where she didn't look for him in a crowd.

Why was it all coming back again?

He'd hurt her. He'd mishandled the trust she placed in him, dashing off to chase dragons and never once coming back to Sonoma County to even attempt to look her up. Not that she was waiting for him. She would never trust a man again like she'd trusted him. Never.

It left her certain she could not rely on her own instincts when it came to men. And here, tonight, as angry as she'd told herself she was vowing some kind of satisfying revenge for his despicable behavior, it was damned hard to pull away. But she had to. She'd never stoop that low or let him see the pain he'd caused. Admit the gallons of tears she'd shed before she learned to live with the fact that she'd never see him again. The emotional rollercoaster in the aftermath of his sudden leaving and the vacancy he left behind made her feel like he'd robbed her twice.

Yes, it was *all* his fault.

It was painful to recall the year she spent along the Oregon coast, staying with new friends until she could bring herself to get back in school. She got her teaching credential nearby in a small town close to Medford and considered settling in a little town near McMinnville where her mother had gone to school. The days were pleasant and the nights cold, but after having difficulty finding anything other than a preschool teacher or daycare worker, even with her Masters', she took fill-in teaching assignments, hoping to be hired for something larger than a twenty or thirty percent job-sharing situation. And then one day, she watched a TV program about the beaches and sunshine in Florida—a place as far away from that tough year in Oregon as she could travel.

The Gulf was to be her second chance. She told herself every day it was her lifeline. The old hurts of the past would just disappear with each swim in the bay, with every walk on the beach, and with the inhale of the calming sea breeze. She was restored, refreshed, her lungs filled with freedom and future, and she found that strong, successful, and confident woman she always knew she was.

But here Damon was, inserting himself into her life again. By accident. Not on purpose, which was the real problem with it all.

Her body was glad to see him even if her heart was sore and bleeding and her brain screaming *'Run! Run away now!'*

If she wasn't in Kaitlyn's wedding party, she'd do what her brain was trying to convince her was the only way to protect herself. But her fellow teacher and friend, who had helped nurse her back and been there while she cried herself dry, deserved more than her desertion. Kaitlyn was one of those women who showed empathy and compassion without knowing every detail of her life's drama. She was grateful for her kindness and patience. And for her discretion not to pry where she wasn't welcome. Some things just couldn't be said, maybe ever.

Martel was dreading the wedding and the reception now more than anything else she'd ever done. Maybe she could talk to Greg or whisper to Brian that she didn't want Damon there. Let the men in their circle of friends handle it for her. Or maybe it would be best to just tackle it head-on and tell him how uncomfortable she was around him.

Martel sighed, raising her head to watch couples walk from the restaurant hand in hand. Her beautiful dress and the makeup and hair appointments she was so looking forward to indulging herself in were just pieces of equipment to prepare herself for battle. If she collapsed, if she let him take away this too, she knew she'd regret it the rest of her life. And maybe she should just let him have what he so richly deserved—a boiling well-crafted piece of her mind. A sharp, pointy end of her opinion she could hurl like a spear. She could do it publicly, if she had to. As long as it didn't ruin Kaitlyn and Greg's wedding.

She drove home, following along the little two-lane freeway, the vein in the archipelago along the beach cities of Madeira Beach, Treasure Island, St. Pete's, and Sunset Beach until she reached her beach bungalow, her refuge. She threw her purse and keys on the kitchen table, kicked off her shoes, and walked through her tiny living room to the sliding glass door and the beach beyond. The white sand looked almost fluorescent in the moonlight. The moon was doing a fan dance with big puffy clouds hinting at some midnight rain like a Rubenesque model.

As long as the sun came up tomorrow, like in the musical score, everything would be okay. The beach had a way of healing the impossibly wounded.

It was too cool for a midnight walk on the beach, but she threw her grandmother's quilt around her shoulders, donned her pajamas and ran all the way to the surf, letting the frigid water spray up her legs and get the flannel wet.

With her hair blowing in her face, she kicked sand into the shallow tide with her toes, first the right and then the left. She felt pieces of shells beneath her feet and stooped, putting a handful in her pants pockets then throwing them two or three at a time into the spray. With darkness shrouding her, she lost her balance and fell to her knees just before the surf showed up to dutifully attempt to wash her back out to sea.

She screamed, but no one came to her aid. The constant, lapping waves made fun of her and didn't give up a soul. Checking to the right and then the left, she knew she was all alone with the powerful gulf. Gazing back toward her house, the fireplace lights welcomed her to the warmth of her bungalow's interior. She rose, soaking wet and full of sand.

Tomorrow was another day, and she vowed to make it stress-free. The wedding was two days after that. In the meantime, she was just going to concentrate on the primping, plumping, plucking, and tanning herself to perfection.

She was going to be the most perfect maid of honor who ever walked down a sandy wedding trail, intending not to pay even the tiniest bit of attention to a man who had his chance once and blew it.

Martel was going to make sure he paid for that mistake with unrelenting coolness a snowman would envy.

SHE WAS THE last to join Kaitlyn's wedding party mani and pedi. All eight of them sat in their motorized backslapping, butt-squeezing captain's chairs with the bubbly jets so fierce she couldn't hear the local gossip. The Vietnamese attendants shouted commands at each other while they worked.

"I'm having a Brazilian," Kaitlyn announced to her court. "Who's had one?"

Martel was the only one who didn't raise her hand.

"You're getting one too. It's on me!"

Whatever a Brazilian was, Martel was getting no clues from the faces of the other bridesmaids. "Just what exactly *is* a Brazilian?" she finally asked.

The titters were so thick they nearly stuck like spaghetti sauce on the walls of the little salon.

"They make you hairless. You get waxed, Martel, down there," one of the ladies pointed to her lap and then gushed a mischievous smile.

"That sounds like it would hurt," she answered the group.

The attendants were carrying on a conversation all their own, interspersed with laughter. She suspected the bridal party discussion translation was great entertainment for them.

"Oh no. Not really," said one of the ladies on her right. "They use special wax; even softer than the stuff they use on your lips and chin."

Martel felt her upper lip and chin to see if she could find any witchy hairs and didn't. "Never done that either. My part-Native American heritage comes in handy. I don't even have to shave my legs."

"Yeah, but just wait until they turn you smooth as a baby's bottom. It feels quite sexy, honest," Kaitlyn announced with a wink.

An hour later, her red fingers and toes looked spectacular. She was called to a small broom-closet type space Kaitlyn had just emerged from for her waxing experience.

"You take *eberything* off from the waist down. Put this on top," she said as she handed Martel a blue paper sheet. "I be right back."

She did as she was told. When the young girl returned, she spanked the massage table.

"Up. You sit here."

Martel hoisted herself up, modestly covering her bare private parts, and lay back, her head on a pillow provided. The attendant nearly tore the sheet from her clenched fingers, pressed the soles of Martel's bare feet together, and then pushed her knees down to the sides as far as she could stretch.

"You hold down. Press knees hard and out to the sides. Make a big smile."

A big what?

Having a strange woman standing over her, staring down at her fully exposed clitoris and lips of her sex, while she applied warm wax with a tongue depressor was embarrassing as hell. But this soon went flying out the window when a gauze strip was pressed over the warm wax and, after a few seconds, ripped away.

Martel sat straight up. "Oh. My. God." It was everything she could do not to scream.

"Only bad the first time. Each time better. You'll see."

At this point, Martel was positive this visit would be her last. The attendant gently pressed her head back to the pillow so they could finish. With each successive rip of the gauze, the pain grew, since much of the sensation was caused by the anticipation and not necessarily the sting itself. And then the humiliating task of having the girl pluck stragglers not picked up by the waxing was the cherry on top.

She was covered with an antiseptic of some kind then powdered with something medicated. Martel imagined her now pulsing private parts looked like a gaping pear-shaped beignet covered in powdered sugar.

"Well? Wasn't that divine?" Kaitlyn asked as she handed the attendant a credit card.

"You are the biggest liar," Martel said to the bride. "*All* of you are liars!" Martel scolded as she glanced into the faces of the laughing ladies.

The bride whispered in her ear, "Yeah, but you're going to be touching yourself all night long unless you get some help with it." Her eyes flashed. It was hard for Martel to remain angry for long.

"No pain, no gain," someone else commented.

Martel wanted to slap her.

CHAPTER 3

EVEN THOUGH DAMON was technically a sailor, ships had always made him seasick. He doubted he could ever go on a cruise. He used beers to hydrate between heaves. It didn't help that the six other guys who went out on the fishing charter were remarking all morning how quiet the ocean was.

Fuck them.

He was so miserable he nearly threw himself overboard just to get it over with.

They pulled up to the pier after their successful day, everyone carrying a bucket filled with fresh fish they were going to have a local bar prepare and serve for dinner. Damon was empty-handed.

"Hey, that's okay, dude," one of Greg's friends said. "My dad was an ironworker in New York when he was young. He told me those buildings used to sway back and forth and not many could handle it up forty stories. He had the kind of stomach to watch a bullfight and eat a tuna fish sandwich at the same time. But take him out on the ocean? Forget it. He would puke his guts out for days."

The visions and just the mere suggestion of eating fish and being sick again was too much for Damon to handle, and he dashed for the bar's restroom, heaving all over the dumb shit who was just coming out of the men's room.

As a result, he fell on the slippery floor and nearly concussed.

Disgusted with himself, he attempted to clean it up, after crawling to the kitchen and stealing a wet rag he found until a buxom barmaid quietly helped him. Her soft, scented chest and gentle demeanor made him almost propose to her on the spot. She placed her hands on his shoulders and sat him back against the hallway wall. She had a Tinkerbell tat on her left breast.

"You're in no condition to do this. Just take some deep breaths, close your eyes, and let me fix all this."

He couldn't speak, he was so grateful. Her little name tag bounced on her chest as she quickly worked.

"Julie. You're Julie," he muttered.

"That's right, sugar. All day and all night." She blushed.

He thought that was funny and started to laugh, until Greg and Renny appeared. The next thing he knew, he was posing for cell phone photos with the girl. He didn't even have the energy to protest.

"How the hell did you become a SEAL if you can't hold your cookies on a calm day?" Greg asked.

"You're a SEAL?" the barmaid whispered, reverence thick in her throaty voice.

He was getting snarkier by the minute and wanted to strike back at someone. Greg seemed like the best target.

"Because, asshole, I spend most of my fuckin' time jumping out of airplanes at night, getting shot at, or capturing bad guys who like to prey on women and children." He followed it up with the best glare he could muster, until he felt his eyes cross.

"Oh. My. God. Thank you for your service," Julie whispered, following it with a wet kiss and a little tongue action inside his ear. He felt somehow violated but couldn't remember why. The day was just going to continue into one big nightmare that would never end.

He'd learned long ago that when things were going from bad to worse, the best thing to do was just go with the flow. When he got back to the table, he took his shirt off and rinsed it in the pitcher of ice water they'd been served at the table, much to the horror of his drinking buddies, who separated like oil in water. Spreading the wet T out on the back of his chair, he sat bare-chested, showing off his new African tats, including the one with Charlene's initials. He drowned his sickness and his shame with the hoppy pale ale he was growing to love.

The men in the wedding party started introducing him to every female who walked past their table. Despite his protests, they told every one of them that he was in the process of getting divorced and was looking for a hot lay.

"Fuckers!" he finally said as he finished off the pitcher, letting excess beer run down his front. He sat back in the chair and nearly had a heart attack when his warm back hit the ice-cold T-shirt he'd rinsed.

"Arrgh!" he yelled. He didn't have to look up to see the heads turning all over the bar. The corners of his eyes caught everyone.

He wanted to go home.

"Should we call you an Uber?" Renny asked, stifling a grin.

He started to answer when he heard Julie interrupt behind him.

"I get off in about fifteen minutes. I can take him home, if you like" She leaned over, her face and lips too close for him to focus. "It would be my honor." Her timbre got very low and sounded a little stormy. Dangerous.

His insides were telling him it was a bad idea. His brain was telling him that his strength was that he could just accept life the way it had been dished to him.

It also was the reason he probably would never be promoted. They would always want him as a valuable and creative part of the Team, but he'd never make a leader they would follow into battle.

He decided to embrace his faults.

"Thank you, Julie. I'll be right here, waiting for your chariot."

He knew all of this was going to get back to everyone else on Team 3 when he returned to California, and he decided he didn't care anymore. He reminded himself of his lofty goals in coming out to Florida in the first place.

Expunge the memories of Charlene from his brain.

Like the conquering hero he wasn't tonight, he got a standing ovation by the entire audience at the Catfish Bar and Grille as Julie helped him out the front door, her arms around his waist as she whispered, "You're doing fine. Just a few more steps."

It was going to be all over Facebook tomorrow. Not his account, because they couldn't have an account due to what they did. But it would be plastered everywhere else, from Florida all the way to California.

He hoped Charlene saw it.

HE COULDN'T REMEMBER the house number of their cottage on the beach, so Julie suggested he sleep it off at her place. He was unable to protest much.

She lived in an ocean-front condo, about four floors up from the sand. It was an older building but had been remodeled, and, thank God, it had an elevator, or he'd be sleeping on the beach like a vagrant.

He headed for the door to the balcony overlooking the bay, but she quickly redirected him to the bathroom.

"You're not to get anywhere near that balcony until you sober up some."

He wasn't going to argue. She was cute and probably ten years younger than he was. Well, she had to be twenty-one at least to work there, so nine younger then. He loved basking in the attention she poured over him. There was a story there somewhere, he thought as he allowed himself to be dragged to the shower that was already running warm and steamy.

"You get those smelly clothes off, and I'll put them in the wash for you."

He was liking the opportunity to mess with her. "Then I'll be naked. I'm shy when I get naked."

She grinned, unbuttoning his jeans and expertly sliding her hand inside to massage his package. "Well then, we'll have to do something about that, won't we?"

Her eyes locked hard on him as she stripped his pants all the way to his ankles. His red, white, and blue starred boxers went too.

Under the spray of the shower, he began to sober

up. He scanned everything that had happened over the past hour or more, and something made him tear up. Where was all this sadness coming from? His chest hurt.

He was really good at his job, and he loved being a SEAL. It was everything else in his life that was fucked up. He attracted women for all the wrong reasons. The women he was attracted to wouldn't have him. And the real gems, well, the ones worth loving, he didn't want to disappoint, so he just walked away. Yes, he was good as a SEAL. He was an outstanding Team Guy. But that was all he was. Everything else scared him into inaction.

The water turned ice cold, he'd been standing there so long thinking.

This is a bad sign, Damon. Thinking will get you killed. And on top of being sick, you're crying like a pussy.

Tonight, he was finding it hard to run away from things that just kept coming back again and again.

This must be what they call Karma.

He turned off the water and grabbed a pink flower-scented towel Julie had left for him on the toilet lid. He dried his hair and looked in the mirror.

Do I look harder? Who was it said that?

It was Martel, dancing under the twinkle lights, the band guitarist watching her every move as she carefully replaced Brian's hands into more appropriate locations. The guitarist smiled, and so did Damon.

He remembered those hands on his body, the big brown eyes staring up at him, terrified as he took her across the threshold into womanhood.

"Love you, sweetheart," he'd said.

"All for you, Damon. Take me. I want it to be you. Make me a woman."

He never got tired making love to her. He could go all night long, because it made him feel so good. He'd forgotten how wonderful she made him feel. Her little kisses and sighs, how her body tasted, and how she asked him to teach her...

He looked back into the mirror. God, he'd been a fool. She'd made him feel so good he didn't ever consider *her* feelings. He knew she expected more than he gave. He knew that's what he was going to do all along, and he just couldn't stop.

He intended to touch base after Basic. After he qualified. After his first work-up. Each time he thought about coming back to see her, and yes, apologize.

Until it was time to leave for Africa. That changed everything. That four-month deployment wound up being nearly an eighteen-month tour. Half the time he wasn't sure they'd make it out alive. He didn't want anyone waiting for him. He had to push out all distractions to stay alive.

So, to avoid breaking her heart, he broke it anyway.

He let the tears stream down his cheeks and drop onto his chest. He let himself see the raw pain that, even though he'd done his job, he wasn't a real man inside. Common, ordinary men could fall in love and take care of their women.

He could not.

He wasn't sure what he'd tell Julie but taking advantage of her wasn't something he wanted to do tonight.

He slipped into her sheets, pink with little dark pink and rose-colored flowers along the hemline and smelling like a Spring day in a flower shop. A light shone from the hallway, illuminating the picture of a young man in a Marine uniform on her bedside table. Beside it was a picture of Julie with her parents and this young Marine.

They appeared to be nice people. Their faces were decent, the photographer obviously posing people not used to having professional pictures done. They were uncomfortable with the process, he could tell, but making a memory to last for generations to come. Making a statement, "We were here. We were all together here."

These were the people he was sworn to protect. He looked into the eyes of her father. He couldn't take advantage of this man's little girl.

He'd never thought this way before.

IT WAS DARK when he awoke, hearing Julie's quiet sobs. He moved toward her in the bed and found her also naked.

"Hey, what's the matter?"

She jolted at first. "I'm sorry. Sometimes I have nightmares. I didn't mean to wake you."

She wrapped her legs around his hips, holding him like a scissors between her thighs. He brought his arm up around her shoulder and let her soft cheek feel the beating of his heart.

"It's okay. You're safe with me. No one's going to hurt you while I'm here, Julie."

At first, she inhaled sharply, then let it out, and then gulped in air again.

He placed his palms at the sides of her face, pulling her up so he could see her eyes and her glistening cheeks and rubbing her temples with his fingertips. "Shhh, it's okay. Honest."

"I'm so sorry. I just get sad sometimes," she whispered tentatively.

"I do too. I think about all the dumb stuff I've done, did tonight, and I don't—"

He stopped, pulling her down to his lips and gave her a gentle kiss. He rubbed his palm over her forehead, petting her silky dark hair. "You're beautiful,

Julie. I imagine you make your father proud."

She sat up. He traced down her spine with his forefinger.

"You okay?"

"That's the third time you've asked me that." She sighed. She was fiddling with her fingers, looking down at her lap. "I need to come clean with you."

Damon's antennae shot up, and he suddenly worried he'd miscalculated everything. *Another exercise in being a jerk.* With one arm covering his forehead, he gently patted her back.

"Tell me, Julie. Just say it."

She rolled onto her belly beside him, her arms out in front, resting on her elbows. "I'm a virgin, and I thought—"

His heart raced. This was exactly what he didn't want to hear. Again, his head was screaming, *"Run!"*

He took several deep breaths and found the strength to ask her, "You thought what?"

She looked at him, even though most of her face was in shadow. "I thought that maybe if you were drunk enough, you'd agree to be my first. It would be my honor." She examined her hands again. "And I thought you'd be gentle with me."

He brushed the hair from her cheek with one hand. He let his forefinger rub gently across her lips.

"Listen very carefully, Julie. That should be something you save for someone you love very much. And when that happens, when you both love each other, then it will be gentle, and it will be the most beautiful thing in the world. Because that's the way it should be."

He saw he'd made her cry.

"I don't want to hurt you. Thank you for the offer. It truly means a lot to me that you ask. In my younger days, with a pretty girl like you—"

Even in the dark he could see her shy smile.

"I would have taken you up on it in a heartbeat. But you're too special, Julie. Making love is more than screwing or getting something out of the way. It's about opening up your whole world to another person, or at least it should be."

She brushed the tears from her cheeks and chuckled. "Well, I was willing to pretend, at least."

"For me? You'd do that for me?" he grinned.

She nodded. He smiled.

"You are special. That's the nicest thing anyone"— and then he remembered Martel—"well, almost anyone has ever offered me."

He gazed at her face, unable to read her eyes. He liked the man he was being right now.

"As much as I'm sure I'd enjoy it, I'd rather be truthful and honest, instead of pretending. I don't want to take the place of a gentleman someday who deserves the honor of your body with all the love and honesty I can see you have to give. It's a beautiful thing, Julie. You're an amazing, brave, and honorable woman. You deserve more."

She started to answer, hesitated and then sighed. "I wanted to thank you for your service. I lost my fiance overseas two years ago. I say good night to him every night."

"The Marine?"

"Yes. He was like you. He didn't want to do it until we were married."

"Well, I didn't—" He had to stop himself. "That's a beautiful story, Julie. You're keeping his honor. See? We both did the right thing…"

She laid her head against his chest again and several minutes later was snoring fast asleep. He enjoyed the feel of her unspoiled body against his own. Her glowing soul warmed him as they breathed in tandem. He couldn't believe what he'd just experienced. He wanted her respect more than he wanted to sleep with her. Her naivety made her vulnerable and he didn't want to take advantage. He didn't want to rob her of the fairytale. Besides, she could always tell her friends she'd slept with a SEAL. And it would be the truth.

Sweet, young Julie had taught him a huge lesson.

About himself.

CHAPTER 4

MARTEL HAD NEVER worn a powder blue cocktail dress before. She also never wore a pillbox hat with a small veil, covering just below her chin. She lost the battle with Kaitlyn, arguing that she wanted to wear her hair long. But it was Kaitlyn's wedding, and the bride had all the young women wear their hair up in French twists at the top of their heads. Martel was the only one who wore a hat and veil, as the maid of honor.

"You look like mother," she said to the mirror. A tiny wave of worry crossed her mind as she hoped she didn't look too matronly. The purpose of the facials, the painted toes and fingernails, the professional makeup artist, and the hairstylist were to make her look stunning.

Well, that's the bride's decision to make and hers alone.

Kaitlyn would be the star of the show, no question about that. Martel just didn't want to show up looking like her mother, like anyone's mother.

All the girls gathered in the pastor's study. Someone had brought champagne, and Martel grabbed a glass, downing it quickly. It did settle her nerves a bit. The bride sashayed next to her, looking sparkly and fresh. Her long blonde hair curled in soft ringlets, falling all over her shoulders and halfway down her back. It was how Martel had always thought she wanted to look as a bride.

"You look smashing, Martel." Kaitlyn's blue eyes were highlighted with light blue eyeshadow contrasting her pale pink lipstick.

"You don't think this hat and veil make me look too old, do you?" she asked Kaitlyn.

"No!"

Several of the other girls joined their circle, each dressed in a different pastel shade of the same style.

"You can take the hat off, if you don't like it."

Martel could see Kaitlyn was trying to please her but didn't really want her to mess with the costume.

"It's your day, Kaitlyn. I'd wear a bathing suit down the aisle if you asked me."

There was a collective "whoa" from the bridesmaids. More champagne was poured, glasses clinked, and they all started bantering like a bunch of chickens.

Pretty girls and idle gossip. They go hand in glove.

Kaitlyn's mother entered the room, and everyone

ceased talking. It would be hard not to notice how thin she'd gotten just in the few months since the original wedding plans were started. The wig she wore over her bald head, due to the cancer treatments, was for a much younger woman. Martel could almost envision a bow of some kind on the side, more of a '60s style hairdo baked in.

She batted her hairless eyelids and smiled at her beautiful daughter, her cheekbones high, yet revealing gaunt and sunken flesh beneath.

"Sweetheart, I've dreamt about this day for many years. I'm so happy I lived long enough to see you married. I couldn't be happier with Greg as my new son. Thank you."

Kaitlyn was a bundle of tears, collapsing into her mother's arms. Her veil, with tiny star-shaped crystals sewn in, got temporarily entangled in her mother's wig, and threatened to push it askew. Mrs. Carrington was quick to stop the movement.

HER MOTHER LOVINGLY smiled at all the girls. In her right hand she carried a pink bag. To each of the bridesmaids she handed a small package wrapped in pink tissue. To Martel, she handed a tissue wrapped in blue.

"These are from me to all of you. Thank you for agreeing to be part of this special day. I know Kaitlyn and Greg are so delighted we could all share this together. I hope you enjoy these little trinkets and remember this special time and how happy you have made us."

As Martel and the other bridesmaids opened their packages, each found a gold heart on a delicate chain, the backside of the charm engraved with the date of the wedding. They helped each other put the necklaces on and, one by one, gave Mrs. Carrington a hug.

It was a sweet gesture, but so sad. Martel missed her mother's presence as she fondled the heart-shaped necklace around her neck and looked into the eyes of the woman who probably wouldn't make it to Kaitlyn and Greg's first anniversary.

"Thank you, Mrs. Carrington. Your daughter must be such a gift to you."

Then Martel's eyes filled with tears. She realized the moment she shared with Mrs. Carrington was something she would never be able to do in her own life. First of all, there was no man at her side like Kaitlyn had with Greg. And Martel's own mother had died shortly after she left for Oregon. She regretted not being able to attend the funeral. She'd told Kaitlyn Mrs. Long had died of a broken heart when her father left the family two years before. Damon had been a comfort to them both right after her dad left. Her mother was his biggest fan, until the end.

Mrs. Carrington knew she was stepping into a role Martel had artificially placed her in. "Your day will come. And in case it's not soon, your mother and I will hold hands and watch from above."

Martel heard the collective gasp as each of the women in the room tried to stifle an outburst of tears. Someone suggested more champagne.

WHY ARE WEDDINGS *so emotional?* Martel wondered. Maybe it was because younger people strive for their happy day, and maybe it was because older folks liked to fondly remember their youth. It was an artificial bringing together of families, made by choice and not accident.

As choices went, getting married probably was the easier one, Martel knew. She'd had her share of choices and had artificially plastered over all the objections and second guesses. Today, they came crashing down on her.

She ran to the bathroom.

What's going on with me?

She dabbed water on her face, trying to remove redness that collected in and around her eyes. A makeup bag was laid open on the counter and she applied concealer under her eyes before adding more silvery blue highlighter on her upper lid. She touched up her lips with the cherry red color she hoped might attract attention.

Well, she was not going to be in her twenties in a few months, as she celebrated her thirtieth birthday. Time to get real. Time to strategize the rest of her story, add some romance, and, yes, more than a little lust. She'd been brave, and worked hard for everything she achieved, covered up her sadness, and dealt with vacant places in parts of her heart. She'd gotten really good at that.

A gentle knock on the bathroom door was followed by Kaitlyn's whisper. "Are you alright, Martel?"

"Yes." She opened the door and smiled.

She had to tell Kaitlyn something even though her friend was too much a lady to pry.

"Just seeing your mother today, seeing how happy she is, it makes me miss my mom." She placed her hands on either side of Kaitlyn's face. "You're so lucky. I hope every day for the rest of your life that you are as happy as you are today. That's my wish for you."

Of course, that brought on a flood of tears streaming down the bride's pretty face.

"It's going to happen, Martel. You watch. It will happen. Do you know how they say, 'the beach heals everything'? I truly believe that with all my heart and soul. I'm so happy you came to Florida and we got to be friends. I hope you'll stay here forever and ever." She whispered, "And I'm gonna need you to babysit."

Martel dropped her hands and stepped backward. "Are you saying…?"

Kaitlyn nodded. "We got a little sloppy. I mean we were going to get married, right? But in all the planning and Greg's job—he's been so incredibly busy. We just got lax and voila! I think I'm about three months along."

"Does your mother know?"

"Don't say a word. We're going to tell her after the Honeymoon, if I can keep my mouth shut." She leaned forward, "I guess they call it a babymoon now."

Martel studied Kaitlyn's tummy. "You don't show at all."

"You haven't seen me naked. I have a baby bump, No question about it."

"I'm so happy for you."

Martel was the last one to leave the pastor's study and was whisked hurriedly to the back of the line to make her entrance after the bridesmaids. Her insides were jumbled. Her ears buzzed, and comments made by the other bridesmaids, the wedding planner, and everyone else around her were muted as if she was listened to them through water. She felt like she was sitting at the bottom of a pool looking up at the world and people performing on stage all around the edges.

Organ music got her attention. Brian, Greg's best man, presented his elbow. "Madame?"

She enjoyed hooking her arm in Brian's, tucking herself gently at his side, as they were given the go-ahead to march down the aisle.

The veil on her hat was scratchy, irritating her nose, and she worried the red lipstick would smear and leave marks all over her cheeks. But she smiled at the audience on both sides of the aisle and decided, even if her greatest fears came true and she looked like a painted clown, she wouldn't let them see her concern.

At the front of the church they separated, and she turned to stand at the left. She held her bouquet of tuberoses tightly to her waist, scanned the audience, and smiled.

The congregation rose as Kaitlyn and her uncle began the short journey to the front. She watched the bride's eyes laser-focused on Greg. She saw the determination of her friend as she crossed the threshold from single lady to a married woman, and future mother. How Martel envied the way Kaitlyn could depend on her man and that he was standing there in front of everyone, declaring his love for her with that action.

Martel found it hard to breathe all of a sudden but kept her gasps for air silent. She had so much in common with Kaitlyn, more than her friend would probably ever know. Her life was going to play out differently. She made peace with it, which settled her a bit.

These two made better choices. Well, even if they weren't better, this day was as the result of their choices. Their conscious effort to design a life together.

Kaitlyn smiled at her through the shimmering veil, handing Martel the exquisite bouquet she carried, a larger version of her own. As the bride turned to face Greg, the couple held hands. Martel was distracted by movement out of the right side of her eye.

Damon Hamlin's steady gaze was not focused on the bride and groom, which would have been much more appropriate. He'd been studying her. And he wasn't afraid to show it.

Martel made her choice. She did not smile but refocused her attention on the ceremony.

AFTERWARD, THE PICTURE taking went on for nearly an hour. They ended the photo session with a mock "worst wedding photo ever," and then the group peeled off and headed to the reception in separate cars.

Brian drove Martel and another couple to the beach that was going to be their party place. The sun had started to hang very low on the horizon, bathing the huge white canopy in warm orange light. The wedding cake and refreshments were set up in the Sunset Beach public gazebo, which was the only part of the reception that was rented. Tables and chairs dotted the beach in clusters. Two large boxes at the entrance were set up for people to remove their shoes. It was the bride and groom's express wishes, boldly printed on a poster above the boxes, that the entire wedding party "go barefoot" in celebration. Kaitlyn and Greg's shoes were the first pairs in the box.

They'd hired a mobile DJ to play dance tunes, most of them being 60s style surfing as well as popular Cuban songs and what Martel called "Margarita Music."

She was shown to her table and promptly removed her hat and veil. She was grateful she could finally breathe.

Several of Kaitlyn's students from their school were in attendance, lined up to give their teacher a hug and shake the hand of the man who had become her groom. She listened to mothers of the children gushing glowing words of praise on Kaitlyn. It was clear, even though Martel knew all about it, that she was a favorite teacher at the school. In fact, the two friends were usually voted most popular.

"Aren't they cute?" Kaitlyn whispered to her after several of her students passed through the reception line.

"Darling. Kate, they think you're a rock star."

"Actually, Greg's the rock star. He has a little group of devotees now. Isn't it great?" Kaitlyn angled her head and squinted. "You took off your hat."

"It was driving me crazy. The veil itched my nose. I thought I was going to sneeze all during the wedding. I'm never going to wear one of these again. Ever."

They both laughed.

She was introduced to several other friends of Greg's, relatives of Kaitlyn's, and other people who passed through the line without identifying how they got there.

She hadn't been paying much attention to who was "on deck," but all of a sudden, Damon was standing before her, extending his hand.

"I like your hair up. Because…" He leaned forward and whispered, "I think you're just as pretty as the bride."

She must have registered shock, because he let his eyes go big, and covered his mouth.

"Perhaps I shouldn't have said that."

"Nice to see you too, Damon." She tried to show him that she had no sense of humor, and the joke had fallen flat. She turned her head to the left and greeted the next person in line, forcing Damon to move to the side.

"Kaitlyn, thank you for letting me crash your party. I like your choice of venue," he said loud enough for Martel to hear.

"I know. It was Greg's idea. Isn't it wonderful?"

"The best." He addressed the groom. "Well, Greg, you got snagged, but I don't see you protesting."

"Good to see you, man. Julie fix all the places that were hurting? You put on quite a show at the Catfish." The groom punched Damon in the arm.

Julie?

Martel didn't pay attention to Damon's answer. The music had started. The line dispersed as the wedding party began mingling with the crowd. Martel left in search of something stronger than champagne.

IT WAS NEAR sunset when they cut the cake. With a swirling, lush orange and purple backdrop, they toasted the bride and groom and then watched the sun melt at the horizon.

She knew Damon had been watching her. She made a point of ignoring him as much as she could, but he caught her sneaking a glance in his direction that she tried to deflect.

Dancing was one of the things Martel loved to do ever since she was a little girl. She danced with Kaitlyn's uncle, and Greg, and several of the groomsmen, including Renny.

"I did not know that you and Damon were acquainted. I imagine you were just as shocked as he was to see you."

"Yes, he's the last person in the world I ever

thought I'd see here. So you guys serve on the same SEAL team?"

"We do. He's been a good friend. I doubt I would've made it out of BUD/S without his help."

"Butts?"

Renny laughed. "BUD/S. Or Basic Underwater Demolition. It's the training we do before—well, *one* of the things we do before—we get pinned. It's that part you see on TV all the time. We have to stay up for six or seven days in a row. You've seen the films, right?"

"Oh yes. I know what you mean now. Tough journey for you both."

"Our class passed about twelve percent of the original class."

"Is that unusually low?"

"Actually, it's a bit higher than most."

"That must make you feel very proud. Have you wanted to join the military for a long time?"

Martel knew the decision had come quickly for Damon and wondered if it was the same for Renny.

"Yeah. My dad was a big fan, a former Navy man himself. He never made it to get his Trident. Sometimes I think I did it for him. Maybe when I retire I might give it to him."

"He must be very proud." Martel knew that Renny was on his best behavior. She wondered how much of her past Damon had discussed with him.

"When do you go back to San Diego?" She was

mortified with her own question and wanted to take it back immediately.

"We got another week. Then it's back to that beach. We call it the Left Coast."

The music stopped, but they continued talking. She noticed Renny was scanning the crowd at the same time.

"Right back into the fray, I guess," she added.

"Not quite. We have a couple special training sessions in the desert coming up. And then hurry up and wait."

"Where do you go next?"

"Can't really say, Martel. Sorry."

"I shouldn't have asked." She shrugged. "It seems like it's so difficult to talk to people socially these days. Between politics and religion and job security and national secrets, everything is so complicated. Everybody's hiding something." Her mind drifted. She felt like she was fading into the horizon, the sun pulling her down into the water.

"Oh wow. Where did that come from?"

Martel shook her head and then shrugged. "I have no idea." She smiled up at Renny and saw a lot of Damon and his expression. His easy-going nature was attractive. She figured not much got under his skin. She imagined it was part of the selection process.

"Now that I know a couple of SEALs, I think I'll start paying more attention. Maybe next time, I can ask more appropriate questions. So, forgive me."

Martel knew that Damon would be curious about her behavior and would probably question his buddy. Feeling on display, she wanted to leave the party, get out of her formal clothes, and get her beach vibe on. Some of the guests were leaving, including several of the wedding party. Kaitlyn and Greg slow-danced as the waves lapped at their feet, getting her dress and his pants wet, lost in their own private world. They kissed, claiming their throne—the King and Queen of Romance tonight.

And they weren't afraid to show everybody how they felt about each other.

Martel was mesmerized watching them, especially knowing about Kaitlyn's secret.

"Martel Long, you've been avoiding me all afternoon." Damon's voice was smooth and dangerous.

She was glad he noticed her cold shoulder. Her plan was working!

She addressed him. "I've been enjoying the company. I'm surprised I haven't bumped into you on the dance floor. Do you still like to do that?"

Damon stood beside her, watching Greg and Kaitlyn. "Yeah. I used to do a lot of things I don't do anymore." He faced her. "I think I've grown up a little. I like to think it's an improvement."

His grin was disarming. She was counting the ways she could try to show him how little she cared for what was going on in his life. It was going to be an uphill battle.

She took a deep breath and tried to sound casual. "I like to think that we are the sum total of our decisions and choices in life. Thank goodness we learn from our mistakes."

They studied one another like it was some kind of competition. Her heart was racing, threatening to leap from her chest and go dive into the ocean. She couldn't stop shaking when his eyes traveled from her face all the way down to her toes with slow deliberation.

"You always liked painting your toes."

She didn't answer him, preferring to let him squirm a bit. It didn't take long for him to completely disarm her.

"Am I one of your mistakes?" His eyes lazily found her face again. His head was tilted slightly to the right, one hand covering his mouth and scratching the side of his cheek. There were the beginnings of a furrowed brow developing. He was nervously waiting for her answer.

"I can't answer that question." Martel watched two pelicans flying low, one of them crashing into the water with a splash.

"Is there any chance... what I mean to say, Martel, is that I'm sorry for some of that."

"Some?"

He stepped closer to her, and she immediately backed up.

"I owe you an apology."

She'd been ready with her answer for years. Martel was sure he wouldn't be. "Damon, you don't owe me anything."

That statement wasn't as satisfying as she'd hoped, but she needed to keep her backbone, demonstrate how she'd gotten on just fine without him all these years.

She was going to leave, but he grabbed her arm, urgently at first, and then released her.

"Let me put it to you a little more directly this way. Martel, I'm sorry." He held his hand over his heart.

She was alarmed that perhaps she had misread his intentions. She was feeling at the edge of some pretty skinny branches, holding steadfast, higher off the ground, about four floors higher than she should be. But the die had been cast. She'd promised herself.

"Like I said, Damon, you don't owe me anything."

"Are you sending me away?"

"I wasn't aware that you'd ever returned. You left, Damon. That was all a long time ago. I've moved on."

He stepped closer to her. This time, she didn't retreat.

"As you should have. I wasn't worthy of you."

"Really? Honestly, I didn't think you even thought about it at all. I figured I misunderstood everything between us."

"I should've done it differently. I'm so sorry."

The pounding of her heart was taking her breath away. She felt him take her fingers in his hand, draw them up to his mouth, and kiss them. He was going to call her to him by slipping his arm around the backside of her waist, but at the last minute, she dropped his hand and stepped to the side.

She made a big show of being brave. She stood straight and delivered her parting thought. "Another conversation for another day, Damon. I'm not ready yet. Not sure I'll ever be, if you want to know the truth."

She thought about her words all the way home. Scenes of their long, sweet lovemaking sessions warmed her, blotting up the pain and loss that was to follow so harshly afterwards. She licked her lips and missed the taste of his kisses. If she could have those kisses back without her having to work so hard to convince herself that he cared for her, maybe even loved her, she could welcome those into her life again, but she wasn't sure she could trust herself to accurately assess her danger or his feelings for her. That young, trusting woman she'd been no longer existed. There were rules—protocol that had to be followed—in order for there to be a relationship between them. Maybe it was unfair of her to require this, but he would have to go there in order for her to keep her self-respect intact.

If he knew what all those kisses had brought her, knew about the little girl she bore for him and then gave away, he would understand. But he hadn't earned that right yet. If he meant what he said, he was going to have to work it out the hard way.

Without her help.

BACK AT HER bungalow, she shed her clothes and unpinned her hair, combing it out. She stepped into the shower, soaping herself off and feeling the touch against her once innocent, now bare sex. One barrier had been broken, and she placed another protective one in its place as the warm water sluiced over her body. She wasn't yet convinced that there would be a second chance on the horizon, even though the sunset was beautiful.

Their daughter would be nearly ten now. She rubbed her belly, her fingers exploring the tiny stretch marks Martel had earned bringing their child into the world. These were her battle scars, not gold medals worn on a uniform.

But just as important.

CHAPTER 5

"JUST FUCKING CALL her. Honestly, Damon, sometimes I think you're more of a girl."

That pissed him off. He jumped to his feet, crumpling the little piece of paper Kaitlyn had written Martel's number on.

"You know one of these days you're going to say something, and I'm gonna pop you right between the eyes, and that'll be it. We'll both get tossed."

"No fucking way asshole." Renny stayed splayed over the couch, still in his pajama bottoms. "You made your bed, now lie in it. I'm here because I want you to stop being such a pussy. She digs you. I could tell. I always knew there was somebody you left behind. Remember? I used to accuse you of that all the time. You were so fucking tight-lipped about it."

"You don't understand," he muttered, gazing out the window at the beach calling him to run away again.

There were so many things that went right the last

two days. And there were so many things that went wrong too.

"Don't understand? When I met her, I said to myself, *'Self, this sweet lady is the missing link. She took a little chunk of his heart and won't give it back.'* Am I right, or am I right?"

He didn't want to admit it, but maybe Renny had a point. He'd gone from one despicable mood to another in the space of forty-eight hours. He'd gone from the biggest jerk on the planet, to doing something he was proud of—proud of the way he treated Julie. And then at the wedding, when he saw Martel again, he thought perhaps this would be the time to do what he should've done years ago. Apologize. That was the manly thing to do.

Except it was so fucking hard.

Well, doing something hard was what they'd been trained to do. *Hard* was putting his body between the good guys and the bad guys. *Hard* was jumping out of an airplane and getting tangled up in your chute. Hard was pulling a buddy off the field, applying enough first aid so he wouldn't bleed out on the way back to medical. Hard was jumping up and running between buildings when he knew his job was drawing fire, so his Team guys could find the shooters and take them out.

But dealing with women? That wasn't really hard. It was impossible. Maybe being so terrible at one thing it made the other thing so successful. He shook his head. No, that wasn't it either. "I can't figure it out, Renny. I'm a fucking mess."

Renny rolled off the couch and joined him at the window, putting his arm around him. "You know when I got divorced, I just decided I wasn't gonna try anymore. Have you ever considered that maybe you're trying too hard?"

"What do you mean?"

"I mean, why can't you just call Martel, talk to her, make a date, have a good time, and give her a good time. That's what it's all about here, Damon. We're just here to relax and let off some steam, and let the girls— you know—have their fantasies, while we reap the harvest. That's what I call it, anyway."

"But I don't wanna live like that anymore."

He couldn't believe those words came out of his mouth. Apparently, Renny couldn't believe it either because he gave Damon that goofy expression that told him he was done talking nonsense. Their conversation was fully bagged, cooked, overcooked, and in the trash.

"I think you're right. You are a mess."

Renny headed to the bedroom and called out, "I'm going for a run. Are you up to it?"

Damon looked at the crumpled piece of paper just as Renny appeared in the doorway.

"Yeah. You're going to call her now. I think I'll give

you a little bit of privacy."

In two long steps, his buddy was outside the sliding glass door, running over the sand dune, and headed straight for the beach.

Damon dialed her number.

"Hello?"

She sounded sleepy. "Hi, Martel." He heard her annoyed moan. "Don't hang up. Just hear me out a bit, okay?"

"Go for it."

"I've apologized to you I think three or four times, and…"

"I wasn't counting, Damon."

"Right. Right. I didn't mean that, I mean, I'm sincere when I tell you that I've had a chance to think about things. And I've grown up a lot since we parted."

"Since you left," she corrected.

"Yes. That's true."

"Glad we got that out-of-the-way. I heard you last night, Damon. I'm just not sure I believe you."

This was tougher than he'd anticipated. "Fair enough. Then would it be possible to perhaps buy you a coffee? Maybe we could talk a little bit."

"Talk?"

"Yes. Just talk. No date. Coffee."

He knew this was the safest option. An offer to buy her dinner might mean wine, alcohol, and who knows what that could lead to or what she might think it would lead to. So coffee was the right choice. He was hoping she was just curious enough to give him a chance to make amends.

He was right.

"Okay, but I have some errands to do this afternoon. Monday is a teaching day for me, and I've got some things to prepare for class. So I could meet you for coffee. But I can't take too long."

"Perfect."

THEY MET AT the Purple Haze ice cream and coffee bar. She wore a bright yellow big shirt that hung off one shoulder, black exercise form-fitting pants, psychedelic-colored running shoes, and no makeup.

She really didn't need any.

"Hey, thanks, Martel." He pulled a chair out for her, and she promptly sat on the other side. "What can I get you?"

"Just coffee. It's good here."

When he returned, she was leaning on the table, her chin in her palm. She cupped the mug with both hands and blew on it then took a timid sip.

"So you just went home from the reception?" he asked.

"I'm guessing you didn't."

"I hung out a bit with Renny and a couple of the

guys. Everything broke up pretty early."

She shrugged and continued to sip her coffee.

He now wished he'd practiced something, because his brain had drained the moment he saw her in the parking lot. He scooted closer to the table, the metal legs on the chair scraping on the polished concrete slab floor. Then he cleared his voice.

He took a quick peek at her expression and caught the remnants of a smirk just before she erased it. It gave him a little courage.

"Last night at the reception probably wasn't the best time to talk to you, Martel. It's been a long time. I never expected to run into you here in Florida. My friends back home would call it dumb luck, not divine providence."

"Cute."

"Thanks, I worked on that a bit," he lied.

She was good at masking her feelings. That was a big change from before. In those days, her heart was transparent and her eyes said everything. Words were nearly unnecessary. But if he was going to do this right, he'd have to make do because he'd blown his chance at trust with her. And he didn't blame her one bit.

"I meant what I said about owing you an apology—" He held his palm up to her in case she was going to cut him off again. "You're probably thinking I'm scheming to get something from you, and I understand that.

Maybe you will never believe me, and that's on me."

"You'd be correct."

"I understand. But I've had ten years to think about things. I should have tried to reach you. And the more time that went by, well, the worse I felt. I did hear about your mother, and I'm sorry."

"Your parents?"

"Yes, before they sold the winery, my mother sent me the clipping from the newspaper."

"Ah." She appeared distracted with something then sipped her coffee again.

"It said you were living in Oregon. I already knew about your dad, of course."

"Of course. I understand he never showed up for the funeral," she said.

"You didn't attend?"

"I was too ill."

"Oh. Anything serious?"

Martel delivered him a brittle smile. "I'm fine now, if that's what you're asking."

"Well, I liked your mom."

"She used to like you too."

"Yeah. *Used* to. I had that coming."

"Can we just get on with what you wanted to tell me, because I've got a lot of things to do?"

This irritated him. She was being very tough on him. But he was smart enough not to show it. "I'll be brief, then." He leaned forward. "What we had, well, to be honest, it *scared* me. I didn't know how to tell you."

"You honestly think this explains things? I can see this was a waste of time."

"I went off, joined the Navy—not because I *wanted* to be a SEAL but just to see if I could make it. I shouldn't have felt that way, but I didn't know how to tell you I still needed to explore that, to see if I was the kind of guy who could hack it. Become one."

He thought perhaps her eyes had moistened up but then decided he was wrong.

"You might have thought it was something you'd done. It was *my* immaturity. It really had nothing to do with you."

Her crossed legs were kicking reflexively, her shoe tapping on the leg of the table. She lowered her forehead a bit and spoke in a clipped, choppy tone. "You don't have to tell me that. I know full well it didn't have anything to do with me. None of it ever did."

She grabbed her keys and stood. That's when he realized he'd just done it again.

"If you say you're sorry one more time, I'll come over there and strangle you. I'll kick your balls and then I'll tie them around your neck. Don't come near me again, Damon. I am so done with you and your selfishness. You haven't learned a damned thing. It was never about me because it was always about you."

He didn't stop her. The black coffee she only partially sipped sat sadly on her side of the table, abandoned. Just like he'd done to her.

He was surprised she even had the courage to have coffee with him when he thought about it on the way back to the rental.

He closed the front door quietly and dropped his keys on the kitchen counter. He needed some of that sand and sunshine, because for all his personal pep talk, he felt pretty hollow inside.

Maybe nobody ever really changes.

He shed his first flip-flop on the sand dune. He took his second one off at the surf and tossed it into the gulf. He watched it bounce, float, sink, and then float again, rolling over. And then the sea brought it back to him.

This time, he cranked his arm way back and tossed it beyond the waves. A pelican was flying low, cruising the shallow water, and crashed down. He came up with the black rubber object he must have thought was a fish. Damon followed the trajectory of the pelican and saw the bird drop it in the dunes some distance from him and fly away.

He looked back at the ocean. He could throw things like that all day long, and that damned ocean would just return it every time. He was playing a surreal game of fetch with an inanimate object.

The ocean didn't react to the sight of the pelican carrying his flip-flop away. She just continued to roll, showing her soft lacy white underbelly, hissing at him, teasing him with the certainty that between the two of them, she was the more constant.

And she'd win every time.

CHAPTER 6

*W*HAT WAS SHE *expecting?*

She had predicted how he'd be. She knew it was going to be a waste of time, but she went anyway.

Why?

Still, it was nice that she gave him the chance. That part of it was good. She'd stood her ground, and he didn't make her shake like she used to. Seeing him so flawed didn't make their situation any better, but it helped her to understand that Damon was just doing the best he could. He didn't have the capacity to do anything else. It lessened some of the anger she felt towards him.

Choices, choices. Everything is about choices.

Her mood brightened, and her energy was back. All afternoon, she stocked up on food for the week She'd bought pens, pencils, and school supplies for her classroom from a big box store and finally stopped to buy herself some flowers from the little Latino lady around the corner from her house. She bought pink roses and scented tuberoses, to match the ones in her bouquet sitting in water in her kitchen.

She thought about Kaitlyn and Greg on their honeymoon in the Caribbean. That was one part of the world she had yet to explore and decided to check out some inexpensive vacation packages for Christmas break.

Now that she'd lost her traveling buddy, she would have to be on the lookout for another teacher friend to travel with.

Her telephone rang. It was Kaitlyn's mom, Mrs. Carrington.

"Well, hello there. You must be exhausted."

The older woman chuckled. "I think I surprised everyone. Kaitlyn's uncle and some of the cousins are passed out all over the house. They can't believe I'm still going strong. Of course, I didn't do any of the heavy lifting, and that's the secret."

"But you must have been the organizer," Martel added.

"Oh my, she hired this wedding planner who didn't know the first thing about running a business. She knew about weddings and was great with suggestions and creativity. But getting all the moving parts to work together? That talent was seriously lacking."

"It turned out beautifully. Such a lovely wedding."

"Thank you. I was pleased too."

"So, what's on your mind?" Martel asked.

"Oh, I can't help it. I was feeling a tad bit lonely, to be honest with you. I was hoping you wouldn't mind."

Mrs. Carrington did sound tired.

"I'm all ears. Do you have any last-minute details you weren't able to finish? I have school tomorrow, but if you need help with anything, I'd be happy to give you a hand later on, or perhaps after school tomorrow."

"No, Carl and the family did a great job with all that. The tables, chairs, linens, and dishes are back at the rental company.

"Based on your flowchart, no doubt."

She chuckled again. "How did you know?"

"Kaitlyn has told me how smart you are. And organized. Said you could have run a large company if you'd wanted to."

"I don't know about that. I was rather proud that I didn't blow up at the planner."

"There's a talent to that. My mother's father was a minister. He was one of those guys who had mastered the lost art of getting people, and volunteers at that, to work together. Every church he ran split into factions when he left."

"He sounds like a wonderful man."

"He was. I spent a lot of time around him. So what

else is on your mind, Mrs. Carrington?"

"Heavens, call me Phyllis. I keep thinking you're speaking about my mother-in-law when you call me Mrs. Carrington."

"Phyllis, it is then." Martel waited.

"I take it Kaitlyn told you about their news?"

"Yes. She told me just before the ceremony. I'm happy for them, aren't you?"

"I'm happy if Kaitlyn's happy. I'm just glad her grandmother isn't alive to see it. She would never have understood."

Martel felt the hairs at the back of her neck stiffen. "She'll make a wonderful mother, Phyllis. She's in love with her husband, and I can see he's devoted to her. Bringing a little one into the world under those circumstances seems like exactly the right thing to do."

"You're probably right."

"Aren't you excited to be a grandmother?"

Phyllis paused.

"Phyllis?"

"I may not make it that far, Martel. May I share something personal with you?"

"I'd be honored."

"I'm being told to get my affairs in order. My doctor says to do it quickly because there's no telling how long I will feel healthy enough to do so. I'm really being very stubborn about it."

"Oh my gosh. I'm so sorry."

"Sorry. How I hate that word. I think they should just outlaw it, don't you?"

"I completely agree."

"There's this little girl Phyllis in me standing in the mirror with her hands on her hips frowning and saying 'no!' She's a very nasty little girl, denying my illness and my lack of a future. That little girl is giving me fits, Martel."

It wasn't what Martel had expected to hear. "So this means you haven't told Kaitlyn yet, is that right?"

"That's exactly right. I don't know if I want to. I don't know if I want to tell the family either."

Martel was alarmed. "But you should. You should be honest with them. Otherwise, don't you think it might make them angry? You'd be robbing them of the time they'd like to spend with you. You're taking that choice away from them. Do you really think that's fair?"

"I wish you weren't right, Martel. How did you get to be so wise?"

"I've made all the mistakes there are to make first. You're talking to someone who is deeply flawed and probably always will be."

"Well, I don't see it."

"Good. I've been working on my technique."

Both women laughed. Her eyes teared up all of a

sudden.

"You know, I used to talk to my mother like this, all the time. I miss the connection I had with her. I could tell her anything, and she'd still love me. She wasn't always happy with it, but I always felt loved. Thank you for reminding me."

"Sounds like your mother and I could have been best friends. That was lovely, Martel. Thank you."

Martel felt something shift inside her chest. It had been so long since she'd cherished anything, felt like she truly loved someone and was loved in return. She let her tears fall without stopping to wipe her face. She made a bold decision.

"I have something I've not told anyone except my mother, Phyllis. With your permission, should I tell you?"

"Well, I'll answer you the same as you did. I'd be honored."

She took a deep breath. "I got pregnant at nineteen and gave my baby up for adoption. It's been one of the hardest things I've ever done. I think about her every day. I can't stop thinking about her."

"Oh, sweetheart. You're carrying that burden all alone?"

"That's the way it has to be. Now you know why I'm so happy for Kaitlyn and Greg. I never had that choice."

"You mean the father didn't want anything to do with the baby?"

"Or me."

"Oh honey. I have a gun. Can I kill this man?"

Martel laughed at the dark humor. "Not if I get him first."

"How old would she be, if I may ask?"

"Almost ten. I've had no contact with her or the parents who adopted her, and that was the choice my mother encouraged me to make before she died. She never got to meet my daughter before she passed."

"I can't imagine a man who would give up his responsibilities like that. That's just unforgivable."

"I never told him, Phyllis."

The silence on the end of the line made her nervous.

"Why?"

"He just left. He left without saying anything."

"That's unforgivable."

"I agree."

"Do you ever intend on seeing her?"

"I don't know if I can, based on how we handled the private adoption. But your secret is similar, don't you think? That's why I'm conflicted on whether or not I should tell him."

"You know this man?"

"I met him again a few days before the wedding.

And he wants—" She wasn't sure how to finish the sentence.

"He wants to have a second chance?"

"I think so. Maybe. He's trying hard. I suspect that if he knew what I'd done, he wouldn't want anything to do with me. You see my dilemma?"

"I think you gave me the answer, Martel. You told me I should tell Kaitlyn about the seriousness of my health issues. What he did to you was unforgivable. So is not telling him, especially since you've now been given a chance to."

SHE THOUGHT ABOUT their conversation all afternoon and into the evening. Phyllis had told her she had to make up her mind what she wanted. The decisions she and her mother had made to send her to Oregon during her pregnancy and then to give the baby up for adoption could not be reversed. She was convinced that it was the best solution for her daughter.

But with respect to Damon, some of her animosity toward him had dissipated, now that he demonstrated his willingness to change. It would be a stretch to see them having a true second chance at love, but was there the space for her to let him try? She had to admit that she'd made choices without telling him, thereby robbing him of being part of those choices. It was too late for that now. But was it truly too late for a second chance with Damon?

Did her anger cloud those decisions? Could she have reached out and somehow found him, even after he'd left? Or did her pride affect the outcome she chose?

She decided the answer to those questions was yes.

That outcome years ago had also changed the life of their daughter. Good or bad, that fell squarely on her shoulders. And so was the choice before her now. If it was possible, should she turn away?

Her fingers were shaking when she picked up her cell and dialed that number he'd called from. He picked it up before there was a second ring.

"Damon, I've been thinking. Could I have a do-over?"

"You know the answer to that, Martel. You don't even have to ask."

"Just so we're clear, could we maybe just be friends, talk to each other? I don't want the whole thing. I just want to be friends *without* benefits."

"I'll take that. I'll take it any way you want."

"No strings. No expectations. No sex."

He cleared his throat. "Is that healthy?"

"Okay then, I'm hanging up, Damon."

"I get it. I really do. No sex. Just friends and see where it takes us."

"Exactly."

"How do you want to do this, Martel?"

"I'll fix dinner. Tomorrow night?"

"We'll watch the sunset, and then I'll leave."

"I can live with that."

"Okay then. And, Martel, thank you."

"Don't say that yet. You haven't tasted my cooking."

She texted him her address and hung up.

What have I just done?

CHAPTER 7

D AMON WAS UP early and took a run with Renny.

"I got to hand it to you, Demon Seed. You clearly have the touch."

"Don't say that. You'll jinx it."

"God forbid." Renny muffled a whistle when two lovelies bounced their way along the beach and right into their fantasies.

"I can't unsee that," Damon said.

"I wouldn't believe you if you said you could. Contrary to what the priest told me growing up, looking is not a sin."

"But you're single."

Renny stopped abruptly. "Whoa there, cowboy. You just wait a fuckin' minute. You're having dinner with your ex and a mighty fine ex at that. You picking out wedding bands and shopping for tuxes already?"

"I didn't say that. Besides, I've got this under control," Damon said as he ran away from Renny. It didn't take long for him to catch up.

"Just what the fuck are you doing? You're like that guy who keeps putting his dick in the electrical socket to see if it will plump up a bit."

"Trust me. I know what I'm doing. We're taking it slow."

"And that means you're single. You look. You're a red-blooded male. That's what we do. That's what we're supposed to do. It's an ancient rite. We get to be all full of testosterone and make them want to drop their drawers and have babies. It's human nature."

"Where did you get all this crazy shit, Renny? I'm learning a whole new side of you."

"You know, I seriously don't think you've been paying attention to me. Like ever. I told you there was something about her."

"Martel. Her name's Martel."

"The missing link."

"You're making me think of an anthropology class I had to take once."

"Now that's not a pretty picture. You like hairy girls, Damon?"

He laughed. It didn't matter what Renny told him this morning. Nothing was going to dampen his mood. She'd opened the door to him just a crack. It was all he needed. He felt like he was twenty years old again, so distracted by her beauty he walked into things all the time.

"As a matter of fact, she's part Native American, and she has very little hair."

"It could all be an act. Women get waxed. Men get clipped."

They both stopped running and looked at each other. "Ew," they said in unison.

They began running again. "At least you're thinking about it. That's a good sign. Just listen to your Uncle Renny, like you didn't do with Charlene. Remember I gave you all that advice?"

"Which advice would that be, Renny?"

"Remember when I told you she liked to spend money? Did you listen? No. Not until your credit cards piled up to over a hundred thousand dollars. Remember I told you when she maxed them out she'd be gone?"

"Yeah, but cutting up the credit cards doesn't work, Renny. They mail new ones."

"You close the accounts."

"And she gets new ones. New joint ones."

"I told you she was always looking in the mirror, checking herself out. She liked for people to like looking at her, and later on—"

Damon stopped again. "Just shut up, Renny."

"Just trying to be helpful."

They continued their jog.

"I'm not sure what kind of advice you're giving me on Martel."

"She's got good spirits, Damon. She's got you being nice to Julie. Her influence on you is to be a better man. She makes you stand up tall when she comes into the room. She makes you feel good."

"I can hardly wait for the advice."

"My advice is not to let her go. She has something you need. Something you didn't even know you needed. That thing that makes you excited to be alive, not wallowing in your mistakes. It's very simple, Damon. Charlene? Mistake! Martel? Go for it, and don't fuckin' let her go."

All the talk about body hair had Damon convinced he needed a haircut and a professional shave.

"I have just the right guy. Greg told me about him. The guy lost his hand in Desert Storm. He cuts hair with a hook."

"No way."

"Swear to God!"

"I'm not sure I'd want him around sharp blades, Renny."

"Oh, he does shaves. Greg said he's got a cute little Russian gal who does body waxing if you want that, though."

"Men get their bodies waxed?"

"Fuckin' A. My ex demanded it for the honeymoon."

"Did it make a difference?"

"Not to me. I guess she liked it. Cost around two hundred bucks too. And three days out, man, did I itch. Little stubble all over the place, you know, in your crotch, under your arms."

"Wait, you got your crotch and underarms waxed?"

"I did. And I can honestly say I will never do it again."

"Renny, why do I listen to you?"

"You don't, remember? That's what started all this conversation."

Sure enough, the one-armed barber did a perfect job with the haircut and shave. He also recommended a local tattoo parlor so Damon could have Charlene's initials altered.

He put on his one good tropical shirt, his freshly washed jeans, and Renny's flip-flops and headed out the door.

"How did you get a pelican to abscond with your flip-flops?"

"It's a very long story and I haven't got the time."

Renny came over and gave him a manly hug. "I'm rooting for you, painless. She says she just wants to be friends, just do that. Make her beg for it, man! You want her so wet and horny she'll be riding your gear shift lever and looking in the kitchen for the turkey baster. Be that guy she wants. That gentleman. I know it's hard, but try for it. I'll bet in one or two dates, you two will forget you were separated for ten years. You'll forget about Charlene, and Lydia, and that Candy chick, the dancer at Lonnie's?"

"Oh yeah. With the basketball tits."

"You've made, by and large, some good decisions, Damon. You just need to clean it up a bit. You get happy, she gets happy. You keep her happy, and you have a good life. You won't have to get waxed or buy her anything fancy or give her credit cards to keep her around. Hell, she might even do housework now and then!"

"Honestly, Renny, I don't think about Martel at all like that. She's different."

"There you go, sport. Good attitude! Just keep it tuned to that channel, and you're on your way!"

With that send-off, he stopped by for a nice bottle of wine and found a pear-shaped bottle of Francis Ford Coppola's "Sofia" wrapped in pink cellophane. It was a light pink rose blend. He stopped by Publix and bought some roses, hoping he made the right choice to bring her pink ones.

Best not to go overboard.

Martel was wearing a colorful kaftan over white skintight pants. She'd pinned her hair up, letting her bangs frame her pretty face. Pieces of her long strands fell down the back of her neck, some of them in curls.

She loved the rose and the matching roses. "My favorite," she said, placing them in water and setting them next to the bouquet from the wedding.

Her house was colorfully fixed up with beach signs and posters. An old surfboard was strapped to the corner by the front door, hooks nailed into it for a coat rack. Yellow lamps in the living room were shaped like seahorses.

Smoke billowed in the patio along the dunes where she was grilling zucchini, corn on the cob, and steaks.

"I don't normally cook this much food but didn't want you to go home hungry," she laughed as she plated the steaks, her other hand clasped around the wine glass.

He helped her bring things inside, and they sat down.

"Home cooking and with a tablecloth too," he said, admiring how she'd arranged everything.

"I'm glad you like it."

They toasted and then dug in.

Renny was right about how he wanted to be a better man around Martel. He noticed he did sit up straighter. He listened more and asked questions instead of talking about himself. He watched the way the little dangle earrings she wore caught the fire from the candles she'd set. The room became washed in the orange glow of a budding sunset outside.

He made note of it.

"Oh my gosh. I almost forgot. We can't miss the sunset!" she squealed, grabbing his hand and the bottle of rose. He let her tug him over the sand dunes onto the warm white sand and the hardened shore. Big white fluffy clouds had morphed into purple smokestacks reaching toward Heaven. Blushes and streaks of deep orange and yellow faded in and out around the sky as the sun touched the horizon.

He was standing next to her when she whispered, "My favorite part."

He'd been watching the side of her face and her hair that his fingers wanted to sift through and re-clasp in her clip. He completely agreed. She was his most favorite part, the part of his life before all the other stuff filled up with clutter and got complicated. She was the tip of the pizza, the center of the cream puff, the first lick of his favorite ice cream cone. She was the beautiful part of the song he played on repeat, that melody in the middle that made the rest of the theme tolerable. The change-up of key, the slight adjustment of pitch and tone that made the world magical and everything possible.

She caught him looking at her.

"You're not watching. You're going to miss it, Damon."

"I'm not missing a thing, Martel, trust me."

She gave him a sly, twinkling look while squinting one eye. "Remember what I said."

"I remember. I remember it all, Martel."

She turned and watched the sun. He slipped his arm around her waist and stood as close to her beating heart as he could, his face next to hers, and watched it with her. She was shaking. Her pulse had quickened, and her breathing deepened.

"Is it possible, Martel? Do we have a chance?"

"The truth?"

"We promised, remember?" He held his breath.

"I don't know yet, Damon. Until then, what I can give you is this sunset."

She pointed to the orange spot that was slowly erasing. He looked for the green flash, and thought he saw just a glimpse. It was fleeting. The orange was giving way to gray. The light blue was becoming indigo. Several early stars came out. People began walking back to the beach paths or into their backyards.

She drank out of the wine bottle and handed it to him.

He drank, spilling a little at the side of his mouth. She watched him, licking her lips, but did not kiss him. With his tongue, he captured the spill and studied her face. He could see from her breathing she was aroused, and it was a thing of beauty.

"Day's over, Damon. Our time is up."

Did she feel his heart groan, begging for her to give him some encouragement? If she could just do one or two little things, he'd do all the rest. He knew he could bring her happiness beyond her wildest dreams.

He took her hand, and this time, he led her over the sand dunes, through the patio and back inside the house.

"Thank you," he said as he brought her hand to his mouth and kissed it. "It was a perfect evening."

He could see the blush on her cheeks from the wine. Her plump lips glistened by candlelight. She faced him, pressing both palms to his and letting her fingers mate with his.

"Say something," he whispered. He held his breath and waited.

Her smile was gentle. "Someday. There's a lot to unpack, all the things that happened in those past ten years. The flight to get here was long, and I'm tired."

He was going to say something like "No need to unpack. We can sleep naked," but he didn't. Instead, he said, "Friends. I've missed you, my friend."

"Me too." Then she added, "Thank you for showing me this side of you, Damon. I hope there's more of that to come."

"There's a lot more of that. More than you'd know what to do with."

She snuggled into his embrace, and he began to feel the familiar magic happen all over again. He kissed her ear and did not follow up with the words his heart wanted to whisper.

I never stopped loving you.

It didn't scare him to feel it all over. She pulled away and dropped his hands.

"This was nice. Let's see what tomorrow brings."

"Fair enough." He walked over to the kitchen and picked up his keys. "Can I see you tomorrow?"

"I'd like that."

"Same time, same place?" he asked.

She checked her watch. "Tomorrow starts in exactly two hours and fifty minutes."

He didn't dare move a muscle. Had he heard it correctly? Was he invited to spend the night?

She lifted the coffee table lid and produced a comforter and pillow. "It's comfortable here, if you want. Or I can see you after school tomorrow."

"Are you sure it's okay?"

"I'm okay with it."

"Will you wake me up tomorrow?" he asked. "I don't want to miss it."

"I'll make sure you don't miss it," she said as she pushed the pillow and comforter into his chest. "Good night."

He was entranced watching her saunter to her bedroom door. Behind that door, she'd be naked. She'd beg for him, just like Renny said. He'd be waiting to show her how he could be gentle and how deep his passion grew for her.

"Good night, Martel."

CHAPTER 8

SHE'D PULLED ASIDE the curtains so moonlight could filter into her bedroom and wake her sometime during the dark of night. She showered and put on a sheer gown with embroidered flowers over her nipples. He would be able to see everything. The gown was only a shadow covering, something to stall him for a few seconds before he unleashed her.

With her heart pounding in her ears, she lay back on the bed, welcoming sleep because it would make the waiting disappear. Her hand brushed across the tiny flowers on her bodice then drifted down to the cavern between her legs.

She wasn't going to touch herself first. Like he had done over ten years ago, he would be the one to open her up again and set her on fire. The pain of knowing they'd lost all that time they could have been together was exquisite. She'd waited this long, she could wait a little longer.

HER CLOCK READ one-thirty when she awakened. The door to her bedroom creaked when she opened it, so by the time she made it over to the couch, he was already awake. He pulled his T-shirt over his head and shimmied his boxers down his hips as she drew closer.

He stood, completely naked, embracing her and letting her feel his hardness lodged between her thighs. He tipped her chin up with his right hand and then devoured her with a deep kiss. Her nipples knotted as she heard his hungry groan. His hands lifted the nightgown and then reached for her, massaging her wet sex, suddenly dropping to his knees and lapping her juices.

Crouching before her, he spread her thighs, running his canines along her soft bare lips, his tongue flicking her clit back and forth, making it stiff and throbbing.

She squealed as he pressed his thumbs against her nub and, with a slow downward stroke, lodged inside her opening where he massaged in circular strokes until she was quivering with pleasure.

"You are so sweet. Oh my God, so sweet!" he whispered.

Standing again, he pulled her body to his chest. His lips still wet with her stimulation, he kissed her. Their tongues played, stroking and darting until he suddenly hoisted her up, wrapping her legs around his hips, and brought her into the bedroom.

Damon laid her down, climbed over her, and peeled back the thin gown. His hands pressed over her nipples, down her waist, his forefinger finding the diamond stud lodged in her belly button.

"There it is. I've missed this little thing."

"I've missed this too, Damon," she said, stroking his shaft, squeezing his tip, and covering it with his precum.

He spread her knees to the sides, dove into her belly button, and sucked the diamond stud. His tongue painted a path down over the tiny stretch marks just below, and then further to enter her again. He looked up, watching her undulate under the gentle ministrations his fingers performed on her. She reached for his butt cheeks, sliding herself down and then rubbing her mound up and down his shaft.

Halfway in the seated position, she was desperate to have him deep inside her. She arched up, and he let her impale herself on him, let her slide slowly until he filled her, let her move up and down on him, squeezing him inside with her muscles.

She leaned back, bracing herself with one arm while she angled herself a quarter turn to feel his powerful thrusts as his cock pressed the insides of her delicate walls. She matched his long fluid hip movements with her own, opening to him deeper.

His urgency spiked her libido, making her heart race. As he pressed his groin into her faster, he clutched her thigh and pressed her buttocks up into him from behind, forcing himself inside deep, riding her hard all the way to his hilt. Just as she was about to release, he slowed, peppering her with kisses, tasting and sucking the softness beneath her breasts, twisting her nipples until they flamed. He covered her mouth with kisses as she arched to press her chest against his, holding tight to his hips with her thighs.

When at last she spilled, he gentled, letting her ride the wave of her own orgasm. All of a sudden, he groaned, matching her pulsations with his own. His sad moan broke her heart as he filled her, holding her still until he was spent.

She drew his hungry kisses from him. Softly, they climbed down together, sweat rolling off their bodies, breathing hard as they collapsed in a tangle of legs, arms, and sheets.

The exhaustion was thrilling. Just as they used to do, she lay with him still lodged inside her.

Before she closed her eyes for the final time, he covered her arms with his, extending to reach her fingers and mate one more time with them, and squeezed.

"Welcome home, Damon."

SHE DARTED AWAKE, worried that she'd miss her first class. She smelled coffee just before Damon appeared at her doorway with a steaming mug. His red, white, and blue boxers were deliciously tented, and he caught her checking him out before he bent over and handed her the mug.

She propped a pillow behind her and raised her knees, leaning on the padded headboard. With both hands, she sipped.

The sex was better now that they were older. And she was more of a participant than she remembered from before.

He turned on his side, placing his coffee on the bedside table and then slid down next to her, his hand fingering the slit between her thighs. "I have to ask you a question."

"Go ahead," she whispered and took another sip.

He stopped fondling her.

"But don't stop doing that, please."

"You like that?"

"You know I do. Is that your question?"

"No, it's not." He rimmed her opening, and she nearly dropped her coffee mug. She bit her lips and closed her eyes.

Damon rescued the mug and placed it next to his.

"The question I have is, did you get bare for me?"

She felt wicked when she recalled the little appointment Kaitlyn had insisted she had done. Smiling, she covered his fingers with her own. "Partly. I did it so we could enjoy it together."

He directed two of her fingers inside, making her arch in pleasure, pushing up. His hot tongue flicked her bud back and forth. She jumped. She felt him move against the back of her hand. She withdrew her fingers just as he entered her one more time.

It was impossible to get enough of him. She considered calling in sick but knew that she'd enjoy the waiting all day until they could explore again. She'd feel her swollen sex as she walked, sat, drove her car. She'd remember this, the way he played with her body and took her until she was ragged and desperate to be taken again. The way he tasted her.

Afterwards, she quickly showered and then dressed. He was waiting for her in the kitchen with a scrambled egg.

"You need to keep your energy up. I have plans for you tonight, Martel."

"I can hardly wait. I get off at four," she whispered as her fingers touched his cheek. She planted a kiss on his lips. "I can't wait."

His hand had lifted the hem of her skirt. His eyes got big as he slid his palm over her buttocks and discovered she wasn't wearing panties.

"Very nice, Martel. Are you sure you're not itching

to stay home?"

"I'm itching for all kinds of things I'm hoping you'll do with me."

His forefinger penetrated her one more time, and she sucked in air between her teeth. She lifted her skirt to her waist, staring down at the sight of his fingers massaging and then losing themselves in the lips of her bare sex.

Kaitlyn was right. She wasn't going to be able to keep her own hands off her pantiless, violated, completely nude sex all day until she came home to him.

He withdrew, slid the skirt down her thighs and rubbed his forefinger over her lips. "Now that's the way everyone should go to work. Wet and full of desire."

"Thank you, Damon."

She extricated herself from his arms and walked to the front door. Remembering she'd forgotten her purse and her keys, she turned. He was holding them in front of him.

"Did you forget something?"

CHAPTER 9

"**H**ONEY, I'M HOME!" Damon shouted as he walked through the front door.

"Out here," came the response from Renny. He was reading a magazine in his swim trunks, catching some sun. Damon retrieved a beer from the refrigerator and joined him.

"Well, would you look at that? You're actually smiling, Damon."

"Yup."

"Come on. I want the deets."

"No can do. My lips are sealed, Renny."

"Now that's a crying shame. Figured the longer I went without seeing you, the longer the very graphic tale of wanton sex and foreplay I'd get. Just what the hell were you doing for the past twelve hours?"

Damon was proud to share what he could. "It worked. Your idea worked."

"Really?"

"It did. We had a nice dinner. We watched the sunset together, and we didn't have sex."

"So why are you just now returning? She throw you out?"

"No, I told you it worked pretty good. We decided to wait until the next day, which was this morning. I slept on the couch and was rewarded with the gift of her presence early in the morning, and we fooled around until she left for work." He took a drink from his bottle and grinned.

"Pretty happy camper, then, I guess."

"Very."

"So, what's the plan?"

"I go back over tonight."

"Have you eaten yet?"

"Just a scrambled egg. I'm starving."

Renny took them to a local burger bar, which sat on the beach at Treasure Island, two towns away. They took a table outside under the thatched overhang, near the railing, watching people as they strolled or biked by. The sky had remained clear and bright blue, nearly matching the color of the ocean.

Renny stuck his French fries in the paper nut cup of tomato ketchup. "So, what is it with Martel? How far back do you guys go, high school?"

"Almost. She was finishing up high school, and I'd just done my first year of Junior College. Neither of us was sure what we wanted to do, although I was thinking about the Navy. She wanted to teach, but her mom was pretty torn up when she found out her dad was chasing his secretary, and he got up and left."

"Hell of a guy."

"We dated that whole year and into the summer. It got pretty serious, hot and heavy. I won't lie to you, it was a lot of fun. But as the months went by, I felt like I was going to just get sucked into all the small-town drama. I wanted to do more than play house, but, dammit, I really loved her. I know that now."

"And?"

"I got this crazy idea about joining the Navy to become a SEAL. This is the part I don't feel great about."

"So, you decided to try out. No harm in that, Damon. What, she didn't want you to go?"

"Nah, man. I never gave her the chance. It scared the shit out of me. I was young, Renny. Real young. I wasn't ready, but I didn't know how to tell her. I did a really shitty thing. I just left, and I left without saying good-bye. I figured I'd come back and, you know, make it right, but I just never did."

"That's pretty cold."

"It was a horrible way to treat her." Damon squinted into the horizon. "She was a virgin when I met her. I told her things to…"

"To get what you wanted."

"At the time I told myself I wasn't doing that. I loved her like a twenty-year-old sex-craved kid trying to play papa, and in the end, I just had to leave it all behind. It scared me. It really, really scared me, Renny."

"Well, did you try to contact her?"

"I did. Right after Basic. I came home to help my parents move. Her friends said she'd moved to Oregon. I didn't have the guts to face her mom. I could have tried harder to reach out to her. But you know, it was half-hearted. Neither one of us tried, really. So, I just felt she was done with me. But I always felt bad about it, Renny."

"Yeah. I have this rule. No virgins. It gets complicated."

"I was thinking about this the other day. In a way, this relationship stuff, not like between the Team guys, you and me or anything, but with women—that's the real hard stuff. I don't give a shit about jumping out of an airplane at midnight or swimming to place an underwater charge. Everyone thinks that's the hard stuff. But that's way easier for me."

"I hear you. That's why I'm not going to get married until I get out."

"Yeah. My marriage to Charlene was, well, it was because she wanted it. None of it ever rubbed off on me. I don't know why I got talked into it."

"I tried to warn you. Remember?"

"You did that. And I was too stubborn to listen. I think I was just a little bit lonely. Remember when we found those girls who had been kidnapped and sold off? The world is a pretty fucked up place sometimes. I guess I was just looking for a little piece for myself. A part of that magic I felt with Martel, to be honest."

"I hope you find it again."

"I think I did, Renny. I'm going to try to do it the right way this time."

"Kinda soon, don't you think?"

Damon shook his head. "I've thought about that too." He stared into the eyes of his buddy. "Maybe I just don't want to lose her again. She's the real deal. I think I'm finally man enough to handle it. All of it."

"A word of caution?"

"Oh, here it comes, that advice I'll wish I had taken later on."

"Can't help it, my friend."

"So, what's your advice?"

"Finish your divorce first."

Damon threw his napkin at him. "You asshole."

"No wait, I'm not done. Sleep on it a bit. Go back to San Diego and really think about if she'd fit in."

"I think she should make that determination."

"Then schedule a meet and greet. Take it slow. Ease into it. Make sure you're doing the right thing."

Damon grinned and had more of his beer.

"What's so funny?"

"That's what *you* told me to do. That's what *she* said she wanted to do. That's what *I* told her I wanted to do. And what did we do?"

"You jumped in with both feet."

"Yup."

They sat silent for a few long minutes. Finally, Renny spoke up. "That's how we roll, Damon. We go all in all the time. That's what we're trained to do. It's a skillset, to be honest. Keeps us alive and makes us more valuable. We're men of action, and that's not just ego talking. We like it dangerous and unpredictable and take command of the situation. Figure it out. Work together for a common goal. Watch out for the other guy. But when it comes to affairs of the heart, well, sometimes it's much harder to hold back."

Damon agreed. "Fire, adjust, ready, aim, and fire again."

"Got that right. Trained to deal with whatever we get. But the ladies are a problem. Always a problem."

Damon finished his beer and stood. "Come on. I think I have to get back. Want to pick up some things for dinner, and then I'll run you home."

"Playing house again, are we?"

"You betcha. And loving every minute of it. For now."

On their way back to the rental, Renny got a call from their LPO, Kyle Lansdowne.

"Got you on speaker, Kyle. Damon's with me."

"Oh good. Hey, fellas, I'm afraid I have some bad news. I'm going to need you back here for the big game coming up. I'm making arrangements as we speak. You'll get the email in about an hour as soon as it's arranged."

Damon leaned over. "How soon?"

"Hoping for tomorrow. I'll try not to make it too early, in case you had plans. I'm sorry. We got too many on injured reserve, and I need you guys."

"Roger that," Renny said.

They both knew the rules. No names of places or specific dates would be given, if it could be helped.

"You guys run into Andy? One of the new guys? He's out there somewhere too."

"Nope, not yet. Is he going back as well?"

"He's staying a bit longer. We may do some quick substitutions, so he'll be coming back eventually, but I need you guys now, unless you've stepped on a jellyfish or fallen from the sky paragliding."

"We did swim with some sharks, but I nearly have all my toes, Kyle," Renny quipped.

"Glad to hear it. That will keep your run times decent at least."

Renny placed the phone back in his shirt pocket. "I

knew I should have muted it for a couple more days, dammit."

Damon didn't say a word. He was recalculating his plan, trying to cover everything in his head he needed to tell her. Renny was right. Things were going pretty fast again. He hoped that didn't doom his mission.

DAMON HAD BURGERS, stuffed with Jalapeno cheese sauce for the grill, a green salad with fresh lemon herb dressing he made from scratch, and corn on the cob she had left over from their dinner last night.

At four-thirty, she walked through the door, surprised to see him.

"Found your key under the doormat. Don't ever leave it there," he said, greeting her with a kiss.

"I completely forgot. I have a housekeeper who comes occasionally." She walked to the kitchen, her eyebrows drawn up in her forehead. "Whatever have you been doing?"

"Just something simple. Are you hungry?"

"As a matter of fact," she wrapped her arms around his neck, "I'm starved."

"Good." He patted her behind and picked up the hamburgers. "I'll put these on, and it will be ready in about ten minutes."

"I'm going to jump into the shower if you don't mind."

"Do you need any help?" he said at the sliding glass door before he walked outside to the grill.

"Always." She blew him a kiss and disappeared.

HE HAD EVERYTHING spread out on the table when she returned, smelling of fresh lemon soap. She wore a silk robe tied at the waist and was rubbing her hands together to finish working in the lemon-scented hand cream.

"I hope you don't mind, finished up your corn I found in the refrigerator. And I warn you, that cheese is hotter than I expected," he said, pointing to the hamburgers. "It's inside there. The cheese mixture is inside."

"Oh. I was wondering. Smells fabulous."

She sat down, lighting the two candles on the table. Damon brought over a bottle of red wine he'd opened and poured a glass for each of them and then sat.

He knew he was going to have to get right down to details so it didn't infringe on some of their playtime.

"We got a call today, and it looks like my stay is going to be cut short, Martel."

She frowned. "No. That's not fair. When do you go back then?"

"Looks like tomorrow."

"Both of you?"

"Unfortunately, yes. I'm so sorry." He reached over

the table to grab her hand. "This doesn't usually happen, or at least it's the first time in six years it's happened to me. Usually we go home, work up, and study for our next mission, and then deploy. And, give or take, we know when we're going, within a few days or so."

"So this means there is an emergency somewhere."

"That's probably what it means. And don't ask me where, because I can't tell you."

"Right. I remember that."

He'd inhaled his food, pushing his plate to the side, sipping his wine, and watching as she picked at hers.

"You don't like the cheese?"

"It's really good. I like hot." She blushed and covered her mouth with her hand.

"Yes, I know you do. I'm glad you do."

He took another sip of his wine. She pushed aside her unfinished plate, picked up her wine, and toasted him by candlelight. "Our last night together at Sunset Beach," she whispered, her voice trailing off.

After their glasses touched, he drank the rest of his glass, allowing the full-bodied red to wash over his tongue, wiping out some of the jalapeno. She swirled her wine in the glass and finished hers as well.

"More?"

"I'm fine."

"Tell me something I don't know, Martel." He finished off the bottle and set them both aside. He took her hand in his. "We need to talk."

"I agree."

She watched him rub and squeeze her fingers, turning her hand palm side up and then down. Eventually he held her hand from across the table and leaned forward.

"I don't want to go. We have so much more to say and do. But one thing is certain, I don't want this to end."

Her warm brown eyes were steady, wide open, and he saw that she trusted him.

"How long will you be gone?"

"Could be a week, or it could be months, although that's not likely. Probably something short, but anything can happen. And that's what I wanted to talk to you about."

"I'll be working until Christmas break. Then I get two weeks until after New Year's."

"Would you consider coming to San Diego at Christmas? Unless I'm not back, of course."

"I could consider it." She smiled.

"I asked you before if you thought perhaps we could start all over again, and I feel like we have. I'd like to keep moving in that direction. I'd like to see if we can make it a more permanent arrangement."

She examined their entwined fingers. "I think that's

going a little too fast for me right now. Would you consider working out of an East Coast team to be closer to me here in Florida?"

"I've got four more years left on this enlistment. I was considering getting out then. It probably wouldn't work to start up with a new team before I left. But we can talk about it. I know you love Florida. Maybe I can make you love Coronado. The weather is nice, but I'll admit this is nicer."

"Do you have these?" She pointed to the bright orange sky.

"Did we miss it?"

"Not quite."

They both jumped to their feet. She grabbed the comforter from the couch and wrapped it around both of them. He slipped his arm around her waist, and together, they walked over the sand dunes and onto the sparkling sand where they joined people emerging from their houses or filing through the beach access trails for miles in each direction.

It felt like they were going on a pilgrimage with all the other sunset gazers, soaking up the magic and majesty of the dying sun, struggling to spread its light but ultimately overwhelmed by the size and tenacity of the ocean.

"It's the same sunset. Just different latitude. Bigger waves. Sometimes a little colder. This beach is bigger with less people.

"I like the sleepy little beach town feel. I feel like I belong here, Damon."

"But you have an open mind?" He studied the side of her face.

"I have an open mind. But I'm a different woman than I was ten years ago. I have this place that I love, that feels right for me. It isn't something I want to give up."

"Don't worry, Martel. I'm never going to ask you to do something you don't want to do. Just think about it, okay? Think about coming out to San Diego, and we'll have Christmas together on that beach. See if we can create a little magic there too. What do you say sweetheart?"

He could see she was thinking about lots of things she didn't want to discuss, and he knew he shouldn't push. He knew if it was ever going to work between them, he'd need to be patient until she made up her mind.

He let her forefinger rub across his lips, her eyes studying the travel intently. She angled her head, watching her movements back and forth until she stopped, inhaled, and kissed him. Her natural kiss was sweet, not urgent. She gave into him then went deeper, as her chest rose, pressing her breasts against him. With the comforter hiding them, he slipped his hand inside her robe and felt the weight of her warm, perfect breast in the palm of his hand. His hand reached down to between her legs, not violating her, but teasing about something to come later on. With her next kiss, she moaned and then whispered into his ear,

"Are we done with the talking, Damon, because I can't think straight."

"Will people be leaving soon? We could fool around here."

"No," she whispered. "I want you in my bed. I want to smell the sheets with your scent all over them so I won't miss you so much."

"I like to be missed."

She pulled away. He couldn't see her full face because it had turned dark. "Only on one condition," she said. "It's only fun to miss you when I know you're coming back."

He stopped. Hesitated, holding her face in his hands. Just so she knew he meant what he said. "Yes. I'm coming back. Nothing could ever keep me away. Will you wait?"

"I did then. Believe me when I say I did. And, I am still, Damon. That's a promise."

They slowly strolled to the house. She blew out one of the candles from the table and picked the other one and walked to the bedroom as he followed.

He checked his cell and saw the text. He set his

alarm and placed it by the candle on the nightstand. The golden glow flickered. In the hush that was the miracle of them finding each other again after so long, she unpinned her hair, slipped open her silk robe, and let it drop to the floor. Her body was an altar of everything that was good, everything that was pure or could be perfect. It gave him strength and passion. It gave him a sense of home.

And he'd worship at that altar all night long, carefully and patiently showing her just how much she was cherished.

And that he'd never let her go.

CHAPTER 10

MARTEL HADN'T HEARD him leave, and she had been sure she would. She tried to stay awake between their multiple sexual encounters. She remembered having him whisper in her ear things that made her blush, that made every cell in her body scream with pleasure. She remembered seeing a slight pinkish cast to the sky at one point and knew she was going to collapse with complete exhaustion. He even kissed away some tears that surfaced, for some reason.

He asked her if he'd hurt her.

"Yes. You went away."

"I'm right here. Can you feel me? I'm right here, baby."

"Yes."

She'd wrapped her legs around his hips. She'd climbed on top and put on a floor show for him, writhing and reveling in the angle of his hips as he carried her, filled her, but mostly loved her fully.

Ardent one moment and urgent another, each time was like she'd never had him before. The more he dove into her, the more she wanted. Her desire for him was outside the human bounds of sleep deprivation, she told herself. She could be this woman he kissed, tasted, pinched, and filled forever. The pain of the loss ten years ago was deliciously adorned in the whispers and fire of this special night.

She was forever altered and would never be the same again. She loved him as a mature woman, not a young woman. With hopeful illusions of a Happily Ever After out there somewhere, not that of a young girl's fantasy.

The sun was demanding, even though the waves lapped on the shore, asking her to sleep on, to dream until her prince came back to her bed. Maybe it was her imagination. It was daylight. Maybe he hadn't really flown back to California. Maybe he was making coffee in the kitchen and had decided to stay behind.

She rolled on her back and felt the throbbing between her legs and how red and swollen she must be. It made her smile that she could feel and would feel for days the result of his lovemaking. It made her want him still.

Slowly, letting the sunlight invade her space in tiny spoonfuls, as if it was lethal doses of reality, she opened her eyes to her new day.

She rolled on her side, burying her head in his pillow, and then held it against her chest and squeezed. She splayed her palm against the cotton surface as if she was caressing his cheek. She remembered he'd begged her to come for him, and she'd done it, watching how her peaking turned him into a man-beast who would take her hard and then ask for more.

She delicately pulled back the sheets, full of the scent of him, and stood naked, ready to face the day.

She needed coffee before her shower. She had enough time to grab something to settle her growling stomach on the way to the school. That feeling of new love deep down in her belly and the heaviness of her eyelids from lack of sleep made her smile. She was still in a trance, drugged with the spell of his strong body calling her to come to him anywhere.

Anywhere?

No. That would be a negotiation. There was lots of time for that.

She started her coffee. Wanting to add some half and half, she dove into the refrigerator to look for it and stopped short, seeing a red can of whipped cream and a note beneath the can.

'Martel, this is for the next time we're together. I completely forgot I wanted to taste this sweet cream between your sweet thighs. Save it for me, and hold that thought I know is going on in your

head. I miss you already.'

She put the note on her refrigerator door and secured it with a heart-shaped magnet.

While the coffee was brewing, she retrieved her silk robe and secured the tie around her waist. She checked the time, and she was okay if she only took five minutes to say good morning to the ocean.

The air was chilly, and a white mist swirled between the houses nestled on the beach and the surf. All the sunrise watchers were gone this morning, giving her the beach all to herself.

Miss you already, he'd written.

Only if you're coming back home, she'd whispered last night.

The warm coffee tasted delightful. She sighed and watched a young family walking on the hardened sand, searching for shells and objects of interest. She pretended that she'd had ten years to teach her daughter how to throw rocks at the ocean, how to stick her finger down a hole in the sand and pull out a sand crab, how to dance in her nightgown by the light of the moon.

What am I doing?

She emptied the mug, dashing into the house and under the spray of the shower after tearing off her robe. In five minutes, she was fully dressed. She put last night's dinner dishes in the sink and added water. She grabbed an apple and took off in search of a bagel and her school.

KAITLYN'S SUB CAME over to her during morning break. "Do you know if she is home yet?" the young teacher asked.

"I think they'll be gone for the full week. They're in the Caribbean."

"Do you have the name of the place they are staying or a phone number?" the student-teacher asked.

"No. She never gave it to me. I think her mother might know. The office would have her number. Why?"

"That's just it. The hospital called. They asked me to try to get a message to Kaitlyn that her mother was admitted. I got the impression it wasn't a very good sign."

Martel had expected this, but not so soon. She hoped Phyllis would last at least until Kaitlyn and Greg came back.

"Let me have it. I'll see what I can do. Did you try her cell number?"

"Several times. I've left three messages already."

Martel figured they were on some day trip or tour and Kaitlyn wouldn't or couldn't answer it. She took the message and walked to a school ground bench and dialed the number.

"Duncan Center," the pert voice on the other end of the phone said.

"Yes. I'm a friend of Kaitlyn Carrington, who is on her honeymoon. I understand her mother has been admitted. Phyllis Carrington?"

"She was brought in this morning. You say you are a best friend or cousin of Mrs. Carrington's?

"Yes, ma'am. I was her daughter's maid of honor. Is Phyllis going to be okay?"

"I'm afraid I'm not allowed to give non-family members much in the way of information without a doctor's order."

"Can I see her?"

"Everyone on her floor is hospice. You have to be suited up to see her, but we can arrange that by the time you get here. Can you come today?"

"I'm a teacher, and I can perhaps get off early, say three o'clock?"

"I'll ask her doctor. When will Kaitlyn be home?"

"She's gone for the week. As I said they're in the Caribbean, on their honeymoon."

"Oh dear. See if you can reach her, and I'll do the same. I'm going to need to locate Mrs. Carrington's Health Care Power of Attorney. Her doctor doesn't seem to have it."

"I don't understand."

"Health saving instructions. That sort of thing."

"So she's not expected to live long, then, I take it."

"Again, I wish I could help. We have the HIPAA rules…"

"I get it. We've been trying, but unless I hear, I'll be by the hospital around three. Phyllis knows me. I'm not asking to insert myself where I wouldn't be wanted."

"I'll try to make it happen. See you later this afternoon."

Martel informed the district office what was going on and asked to leave early, citing she had a film the class could watch for the last hour of school if someone from admin could monitor them. She'd already given out the assignments for the day.

They granted her request and asked to be kept informed.

SHE CONSIDERED CALLING Damon but wanted to see Phyllis first. She also hoped Renny might have Greg's cell phone number, since she didn't know anyone else from their circle of friends she could call.

Adrenaline kept her going. The excitement of her new relationship mixed with the feeling of loss while he was away on deployment and now Phyllis. Everything in her life was in flux. The huge emotional swings would take its toll when she finally had a minute to herself. The quiet, peaceful beach was calling her.

The medical center was a private clinic with lush grounds, resembling more of a country club than a hospital. But as she drove past the tall palm trees, the sparkling water and the bird sanctuary, she was struck with what a beautiful place it would be to just pass away into the sunset.

If there had to be a place, that is.

A large hearse was pulling around the back side of the single-story campus, and she shivered. All of a sudden, the idyllic setting began to feel more like a scary movie where awful things happened behind a backdrop used to disguise their real purpose. She was driving through the valley of the shadow of death, just like the Bible said.

She parked, yet something inside her wanted to run. Was she ready for this? Martel felt guilty, disgusted with herself. This was the least she could do for her best friend, to the kind and gentle woman she'd shared secrets with.

Be brave.

She was directed down the wide hall to the right. A nurse was waiting with a disposable gown, gloves, and a headpiece-type contraption with a clear plastic visor covering her face.

Dammit, another veil!

The attendant slipped blue gathered paper slippers over her shoes and opened the door, taking her arm and bringing her into the dark room.

The entire wall over Phyllis's bed was jammed with electronic devices that beeped, flashed colors of red, yellow, and green. There were tubes everywhere. One connected her to an oxygen mask with straps adhering over her ears. She had an I.V., as well as a much larger tube extending out the bottom of the bed from under her sheets.

Phyllis looked so tiny compared to all the equipment, like she was an eight-year-old who'd just had her tonsils out. Her wig was removed, showing her shiny bald head. But her color was good, and she seemed to be breathing comfortably. She wore bright red lipstick, which nearly made her laugh. It had been applied slightly askew.

The nurse nodded to her.

Martel took her hand and called out. "Phyllis? I'm afraid you probably think you don't know me, but it's Martel. I came to see you as soon as I heard."

Phyllis opened her eyes and started to laugh, then coughed. The nurse was right there, adjusting a machine and repositioning her facemask that had gotten dislodged.

Kaitlyn's mom smiled. Her eyes still had that will to live, that fire and fearless courage Martel wasn't sure she herself had.

"Look at us two, would you?" Phyllis growled. She

tried to sit up, and the nurse stopped her. She motioned with her finger on her other hand for Martel to lean in closer. Phyllis' right hand clutched Martel's and wouldn't let go.

The nurse slid a chair to the back of Martel's knees, and she sat, leaning over.

With their faces not more than two feet apart, Phyllis still insisted on leaning forward when she said, "Let's just rip out all this stuff and go get an ice cream and run on the beach, okay? Would you please break me out, honey?"

The nurse was giggling.

Phyllis pointed a bony finger at her. "You think that's funny? You never know, it might be just the cure I need."

"Maybe an imaginary beach and imaginary ice cream," the kind nurse softly purred in return.

Phyllis dismissed her with the brush of her hand. "Not the same thing. Not the same thing at all!"

"How do you feel?" Martel asked her and then regretted it when she saw Phyllis' expression.

"Like the turkey at Thanksgiving. I've been stuffed with crap, stitched up, basted, and herbed, and I have a butt plug I didn't ask for," she said as she glared at the nurse. "I mean, when I was a much younger woman, I might have tried one, but it makes me itch."

Martel put her hand up to her mouth to stifle the

laughter that was exploding her chest.

"I can't believe you. Your sense of humor is out of this world."

"Yes, ma'am. And that's right where I'm going, too."

"Phyllis, don't say that."

"Should I say, *'Have a nice day?'* perhaps?"

Martel shook her head at the nurse. No doubt they'd been seeing a lot of this behavior.

"Only one way to go, and that's fighting. It makes no sense to me to spend your last moments on earth being miserable, crying your eyes out. Besides, these people don't even know me. They see it every day."

Martel recalled the sight of the hearse driving around the backside of the hospital.

"Well, now that I'm here, what can I get you?"

"How about a young man, like your SEAL friend? I never got one of those. I didn't even know they existed, or else Kaitlyn might not have had the father she did have for all those years!"

Martel was laughing so hard she couldn't see out of the visor. Tiny teardrops obscured what her own eyes didn't.

"Maybe I could find you a retired admiral, Phyllis," she finally managed to get out.

"An admiral! Now wouldn't that raise eyebrows at the Club? Find me a bald one, and we could cross-dress."

"Now I know why Kaitlyn is so normal. You did a good job, Phyllis. She was lucky to have you. I can only imagine what growing up in your household would be like."

Phyllis swished in the air. "It was easy. She was a good kid."

"You were happy," Martel said through her tears.

Martel sighed. She was watching someone leave this earth she would have really liked to get to know. It was so unfair. She rubbed her fingers over the older woman's and then patted her hand.

Phyllis gripped her hand tightly, attempting to lean forward again, and whispered, "Go find your daughter. Tell her yourself what you did for her. She deserves to hear it from you."

CHAPTER 11

THE BASE AT Coronado was a beehive of activity. Renny and Damon arrived just in time to grab their pre-packed duffle bag, stored in the Team 3 building, jump on the transport plane, and takeoff not more than a half an hour after they landed.

"Shit, Renny. Looks like I'm destined to never be able to keep my word."

"She's gonna understand, Damon. You call her as soon as we hit the island."

Everything about the operation was ass-backwards. There was no preflight meeting. There was no explanation of duties. It was just hurry up and get your butt on the plane and the rest would be explained later.

Damon and Renny pointed out to each other the lack of newbies on this trip. There were only going to be fourteen this time, and most of them had been in for ten years or more. Not only that, nobody was injured or recently injured during the past twelve months.

Kyle was going to meet them over at Cape Verde. He was already there working out some evacuation plans with one of the carrier groups in the area. At least, that's what their state department liaison told them.

The rest of the story Damon suspected was just being made up. Nobody really knew what was going on.

They stopped over for a refuel in Maine before taking the final leg across the Atlantic to Cape Verde. A ship was going to bring them closer to the African coast, if that was required, and Damon suspected it would be a halo jump in the pitch black of night or a landing with their inflatables. Either way, it would involve a night landing... on the dark continent of Africa. He'd looked over some of the information about Cape Verde, sure that he had traveled here in the past. He discovered he'd been to one of the other islands.

Landing at the short strip was a harrowing experience. The local contractor brought in the big transport like he was piloting a dust cropper, except the behemoth didn't maneuver anything like a glider or smaller twin engine. They started their approach by clipping a palm tree, toppling it on top of a water truck that immediately exploded, sending water everywhere. He hoped that wasn't their drinking supply.

Crossing his fingers, Damon heard the squeal and

saw the white smoke of the tires skidding nearly the whole distance of the strip. They almost took out an old naval barracks. The transport literally was within two feet of kissing the concrete bunker.

Damon was grateful they had any landing gear left.

After a quick tire change, the big green transport took off again, abandoning them on the dusty hot tarmac. There was no one else in sight.

Damon had read this was the airfield European and US Forces had used to support operations in Morocco and elsewhere, sometimes dropping off humanitarian aid or equipment when hotspots flared. More than one African leader, having lost a recent election, found this to be a point of no return, as he was jetting off to Paris, or London, or the Caribbean, never to be heard from again.

Other than a few rusted planes and piles of parts, nothing looked like it was fly-worthy. Certainly no sign of jet fuel. It was the perfect place to drop the Team and would not attract attention. In fact, this was the part of the island nobody wanted to live on. Rainfall was practically nonexistent. The population liked to live somewhere green or closer to the industrialized port city of Mindelo, where they were told all the jobs were.

A convoy of black suburbans scampered across the tarmac like spiders on parade. Of course, their LPO,

Kyle Lansdowne, was driving the first vehicle. He hopped out, sweat having soaked under his arms and nearly reaching his waist. He barely greeted them, pointing to the other vehicles. The elite squad loaded their gear and crossed in the opposite direction from where they'd arrived, through a chain-link fence that had been partially torn down.

The road was nonexistent. For a time, they traveled down the gully of a winter stream, passing a dead cow on its parched banks. The cow's belly was bloated, and its legs reached for the sky. There were small houses nearby, put together with corrugated metal and rusty wire, but the area now appeared abandoned.

They turned around a former school, covered with graffiti Damon couldn't recognize. Parts of an old chapel still stood in the center of the complex, indicating perhaps it had been a mission school at one time. Its walls were blown up in places all the way to the foundation plates. Rubble littered the former schoolyard, making passage difficult and slow. Several large rocks bounced up and hit their undercarriage.

Kyle didn't take the time to stop and check for damage.

They started to climb, doing switchbacks up the steep terrain, and as they did so had a view of the harbor, filled with commercial fishing boats, small dinghies, and three or four military-style former gunboats. None of it looked familiar.

After another ten minutes, they had traveled half-way up the hillside to the Blue Marlin Hotel, a huge white square structure that reminded Damon of a concrete factory. Balconies had been attached to the *outside* of the building. Holes had been blasted in the walls, to accommodate windows. Around the edges, local craftsmen had wedged small rocks, cementing them to hold everything together.

The Blue Marlin was a poster child for building a huge eyesore out of completely recycled material. It had no redeeming qualities whatsoever.

As if reading his mind, Kyle turned off the engine and spoke for the first time. "Have no fear. It has a pool"

Inside, the lobby was cool. Deep royal blue neon light strips encircled the downstairs, also defining the front of a huge bar made out of black granite. Above the lighted glass shelves containing hundreds of bottles of liquor, hung a large mirror, the edges of which were painted in Parisian Metro-style letters, complete with colorful pre-Victorian pictures of well-endowed ladies in various degrees of undress.

The concrete floor had been polished to perfection. It looked like they were standing on a black glass lake.

Somebody whistled as the team huddled in the center of the room. Damon looked up to find railings and balconies installed on the inside as well, a series of metal cat walks crisscrossing back-and-forth between the floors. He guessed it had been some kind of factory converted to hotel or night club use. He also suspected it had something to do with the drug trade.

"Sit down and take a load off, gents." Kyle barked.

They dropped their bags at their feet. Some men sat on them. Damon and Renny stretched out on the deliciously cool floor.

"We don't have to worry about our footprint here, since anybody who has the technology to pick up a signal would be off the coast. That would be military or pirates. And, in this part of the world, we're talking the same thing, unless they are U.S. assets. We had a drug and human trafficking operation here that we have just discovered, and it's staggering how much money flows through this little shit hole."

He continued. "What you see here is an old brothel converted from a UNESCO water treatment plant facility."

Kyle paused to let that sink in.

A water treatment facility on the side of a hill?

"You will notice the one thing missing here, of course, is water. But the World Bank gave them a few billion, so this is what they got for their investment in the country's economic development."

"Some of you have been to the Canaries and you've

been to Cape Verde before, perhaps. In case you didn't know it, they speak Portuguese and a kind of creole pigeon-English-Portuguese dialect, and when they don't wanna listen to you, they'll make it *real* obvious. Don't worry about it. You won't understand a word if they don't want you to."

The group chuckled. Damon always liked how colorful Kyle could be when he was describing a new location.

"And don't let this place fool you. It's the site of a lot of pain and misery, not to mention bloodshed. Most of the people who died here were young girls. This is going to shock you because it sure fucking shocked me when I heard it. Last year, before they shut this place down, it was estimated they were trafficking more than four thousand girls annually."

Comments from the team were muttered and frequent.

"Right now, this little square of real estate is costing Uncle Sam close to one billion a year. It's not for rent. It's for a payoff. We are given this place and access to and from this place for thirty days and thirty days only. After that, it's business as usual, unfortunately. It's a real Quid Pro Quo, and yes they do exist. Someone got their finance minister and his family out, and in exchange, we get to rent this. You know how it goes, we clean it up, take the bad guys out, and their competition comes in and fills in the gaps, right?"

Most of the Team shook their heads. A couple of the men said "right."

"We'll be talking to the US Carson City out of here when we're done. They'll take us to another airstrip, undetermined at this point, so we can fly home. If we get everything done in a week, then you get to be back before Thanksgiving. If it takes thirty days, then we probably fucked it up pretty good."

"I want you all to divide up in the rooms upstairs, and yes, there is an elevator. There is even a swimming pool on the roof level. Bear in mind, if you were swimming in that pool or laying out next to it, satellites, birds and drones will take pictures of your sorry asses. So, I suggest you swim at night, if we're not working. No, I don't wanna have to remind anybody about the rules. This is a big one."

He surveyed the circle of men. "We meet back down here in about four hours, okay?"

Renny and Damon ran up the flight of stairs to the third floor, having spotted a large conference room with double glass doors overlooking the largest balcony and catwalk. If a room was a room, then a large conference room like this would be perfect for the two of them.

What they found was an executive club level meeting room, complete with another stocked bar, and a see-through mirror between the bathroom and the large king size bed in the bedroom. They searched for a second bed, and Renny informed Damon that they'd have to be sharing the bed.

"Sorry, kid."

"Let's put something over that mirror, because I sure don't wanna watch you take a shit or even a shower," Damon told him.

Renny found a box of tarps left over from a painting crew. "You bring the duct tape?" he asked.

"I sure did. Always, man." As Renny started to hang the tarp, Damon jumped up to help by positioning it. Their divider was complete in less than two minutes.

"I'm gonna give Martel a call, okay?"

"Go for it. I'm taking a shower."

Damon sat on the enormous chocolate-colored leather couch located underneath the largest picture of a woman's boobs he'd ever seen. He outstretched himself, glancing up at the erotic shapes, looking like they were floating all around him, and dialed.

His call went right to voicemail.

"Hey, sweetheart, I'm thinking hard about you right now, and I sure do miss you. We got here, and we're safe. And it looks like it's not going to be a long one. Other than that, I don't know anything. But I can't wait to be back home."

He continued letting his eyes lazily wander over the long circular strokes in the picture and figured out that some of them had been made by a woman's breasts.

"I've been thinking when I get back it might be a good idea to plan that trip. Or maybe I can fly out there, pick you up and accompany you to my humble abode."

He hit the pound sign. It wasn't how he wanted to sound, so he erased the message and started over.

"Hey, sweetheart, we made it over here safe. Renny is fine and says hi too. I'm thinking of you a lot. I can't believe just twenty-four hours ago we were doing some pretty nice things. I hope you found the whipped cream. I hope you think of some good uses for it when I get home. I can't wait to see what you come up with, if you know what I mean. Call me when you can."

He hesitated then added, "I can't stop thinking about you, miss you, and, well, wanted to say… I love you, Martel. I can't believe I was so stupid not to tell you that before I left. But I do."

He signed off. "Talk soon, bye."

He made the sound of two kisses and then sent the message.

CHAPTER 12

S OMEWHERE, HER MOTHER had the adoption papers. She had reduced all of her mother's things to one bank box, much of it mementos she couldn't bear to read, like her parents' marriage certificate, her birth record, and pictures of a family long gone.

Shortly after Phyllis had grabbed her and given her the command, the machinery above her head started sounding alarms, and Martel was quickly whisked from the room. She waited for over two hours and then was told Phyllis was still alive, but sleeping.

And she might not wake up.

Had Kaitlyn's mom expended the last bit of her life to deliver that message? Martel wondered how she would be able to tell her best friend.

A light mist hit the windshield as she drove home.

Heaven is crying.

She didn't want to think about all the decisions she made so many years ago. She was grateful she had her mother's wise counsel to fall back on. But there was one day when she actually came close to contacting Damon's parents, in an effort to find him.

"What's got you so blue, Martel?" her mom asked.

"What if something's wrong? What if he's sick somewhere or had an accident or something?"

"Okay. Then call them."

Her mom was good at not pushing. She stood in front of her with her arms crossed until the weakness in her legs forced her to sit down.

"You have to make a decision, one way or the other, Martel. You lay out all possibilities, the reasons for and against, and then you decide. I know there's part of you that doesn't want to do this. But you know how this story goes. I mean, it's been sixty days, and you've not heard one word, you've not read anything in the paper, and none of your friends have said anything, except that he joined the Navy. What does that sound like?"

She'd been right. And while the relationship with Damon may have been a mistake, her baby wasn't. That little life deserved to grow up and be a shining light for any of the childless couples she'd been reading about. She held the decision to bestow on one of them a miracle.

So she never called. After she made her choice, and the introductions were over, they chose the home up in Oregon, because it was closer to the new parents. Her sole job was to bide her time, get ready to attend college in the fall, and stay healthy.

The day they called her to let her know her mother was struggling and at the edge of her own life, the kind hospice nurse told her that her mother took great pleasure looking at the pictures Martel was sending. She kept them in a leather folder in her purse.

"She wants you to do nothing but focus on the rest of your life, Martel. She doesn't want any shame to fall on you."

"Tell her I want to be there."

"I will, but she wants you to stay in Oregon. She understands and told me expressly to let you know this. I'm afraid there won't be any other messages, Martel."

The private shelter on the Oregon coast was a refuge. The small staff was experienced working with unmarried mothers coming from all sorts of situations. After her mother's passing, they helped her plan the service and supported her decision not to attend.

Martel continued sorting through the papers in the banker's box until she found the leather envelope containing her pictures. They'd been placed in plastic sleeves, organized by date. One by one, they chronicled her development, some ultrasounds, and the view of her body from the side. On the back of the last picture, when she was nearly seven months along, her own handwriting displayed a message for her mother. She'd just gotten the news she was having a girl. Years later, it was now a message to herself.

Very soon now, you'll get to see her.

She was sure her mother was delighted.

Behind the last picture in the box was a folded sheaf of papers. When she unfolded it, she found a copy of the adoption contract, first signed by her and then countersigned by the baby's future parents below.

Martel had never seen the paper after she'd signed it. But her mother somehow had. The couple had only been known to her as Mark and Lori, and she wasn't told exactly where they were from, but she guessed it was some place in Oregon. Lori was a teacher like Martel wanted to be some day. And Mark was the principal of the school Lori worked at.

They really had turned out to be the best choice, the perfect parents. The contract spelled it all out: Arrangements for the Oregon stay, her doctor visits and hospital paid for up front, and her own clause. Everything was there, including that it was her wish not to be part of the baby's life after the birth. The records had been sealed forever, she was told.

Except now Martel had their last name. Newberg. Mark and Lori Newberg.

Should she try to call them? Her mother had thought it best if she didn't. But Kaitlyn's mom clearly was in the other camp. Now, ten years later, her perspective had totally changed. She was warned that this might happen, but she signed the paperwork anyway.

How hard would it be to trace them down? Would she be in some legal jeopardy if she tried to reach out? She just wasn't sure.

A red dot blinked on her cell. She saw that Damon had left her a message.

'Hey sweetheart...'

Before she returned his call, she searched her heart. She was actually contemplating doing the unthinkable. But she wasn't doing it for him. This wasn't even something she was doing for herself. She wanted her daughter to know that she loved her, would always love her even though they'd barely met. The gift of her life was for her.

There was more research to do, making sure she wasn't doing anything illegal for one. She didn't want to interfere with her daughter's adoptive parents, insert herself where she didn't belong. When she sorted all that out, she'd consider telling Damon. If they continued their relationship the way it was planned, it wouldn't be right if she kept him from the truth.

But how and when? That was the real mystery that could threaten the balance of everything.

She dialed Damon's cell. Her heart was on high alert.

"There you are!"

"Here I am. Wish you were here too."

"I'd Roger that. Tell me you're looking out at the beach. Probably sunset now, right?"

"It's been a bit rainy, so it's a little on the gray side. But the clouds are beautiful. Lots of purple tonight."

"Nice."

"How about there?"

"Not so glamorous. It's been overrun with people who were just trying to survive and left in a hurry. The other side doesn't look like such a wasteland, I'm told."

"So, no beach time, I guess."

"Probably not. We're a few miles away. Hey, I found out we can do Facetime calls. We'll have to set that up. Can't do it tonight, but maybe tomorrow or the next day."

"That would be nice, Damon. Just let me know."

He must have detected something because he asked her if anything was wrong.

"Kaitlyn's mother I think is passing. I've tried to get hold of her. Renny doesn't have Greg's cell number, does he?"

"He's not here right now, but I'll ask him." He hesitated. "You knew she was sick, right?"

"Oh yes. It just surprised me. I'll feel better when I reach Kaitlyn."

"You sound tired. You should flip off your phone

and turn in early. Doctor's orders."

"I think I'll have a bath and do just that. How about you?"

"Getting ready for a meeting downstairs. I rested on the plane, so I'm good to go. Sorry that this will have to be a short one, Martel. But I appreciate the update and the chance to hear your voice. I'll text you if I have Greg's number anywhere."

"Thank you. Please be safe."

"I made a promise, and I intend to keep it."

"I believe you. I'm still figuring out what I want to do with that whipped cream when you get home."

"There you go. And we're on for the visit to San Diego?"

She heard some voices in the background before she could answer.

"That's my cue. Gotta go. Are we still on?" Damon rushed.

"Yes. Let me give you the dates I can be there. Are you sure you'll be home?"

"Better be. Okay, they're screaming for me now. I'll try to call next chance I get. Love you, Martel."

"Coming back at you ten times over. Be safe."

But he had already disconnected the call.

CHAPTER 13

"**W**E HAVE A wrinkle in the plans," Kyle Lansdowne started. "Turns out we have a possible hostage situation going on. Senator Raymond's daughter, Samantha Raymond is possibly being held against her will. She was part of a missionary group and aid outreach in Nigeria, passing out Bibles and doing things State didn't realize was going on."

Damon knew this was bad news.

"She's gotten romantically entangled with one of the sons of a very powerful Nigerian businessman, Kwanda Freescott. He's a bad dude, responsible for running arms, embezzling funds meant for domestic help, and we think he's partly involved in the trafficking. We don't know about the boy."

Kyle went on to further elaborate how assessment was that the boy was somewhat naive, perhaps dazzled with the friendship with the Senator's daughter, and had experienced a recent evangelical conversion. But they had credible intel that found the group was going to use Samantha as leverage to get the U.S. to back off their enforcement efforts to shut the cartel down.

"Does she know about the trafficking?" Coop asked.

"We aren't sure, and we think not. The Senator certainly has no knowledge of it, or so he says. Seems that Samantha lives with his ex, who has had some major involvement with a group doing these things all over Northern and Central Africa. Part of their ilk was rescued in Afghanistan, many of you might know, about five years ago."

Damon knew it was sometimes difficult for State to control these groups, especially since the government relied on them occasionally for on the ground intel. The delicate balance was where people were killed and unpredicted outcomes happened.

It would be right where they were going.

"We were prepared to do an amphibious landing in Benin. Now that we understand she's here on Cape Verde, we'll be staying here. And our timeline has moved up a bit. We can't be here very long before we start attracting attention. We are not being hosted by any official government entity. We have a promise of some cooperation, but when the shit hits the fan, you know how much weight that means."

"Any friendlies on the island?" Fredo asked.

"Lots of Europeans live here. Historically, people here actually fought in our wars, including the Revolutionary and Civil Wars, even Vietnam and World War II. So we have some friends, especially amongst the older population. With the reduction in the slave trade during the 18th and 19th centuries, the country, as part of Portugal, fell on hard times. It's had to claw itself back and is still struggling with their new independence in 1975. Eradicating the drug trade necessitates an all-out purge about every ten years. But this human trafficking explosion caught everyone off guard. They walk a line between being friend to the U.S. and depending on support from Uncle Sam, as well as Portugal and Europe. They also have a sizable Chinese population, which is becoming interesting." Kyle paused. "We also think they wish the Senator's daughter wasn't involved, so maybe we'll have some help. We just don't know. What they do understand is that if anything happens to her, all Hell will break loose."

He gave instructions for everyone to get some rest, go for a swim, if necessary, and be ready in the morning for another updated briefing.

"Remember what I always say, don't trust anybody until you see they've taken up arms by your side to defend you. Until then, don't assume anything. If we can negotiate our way out of something heavier, trust me, we're working on it. And no mention of the

Senator's daughter, either, got it?"

The cold fish sandwiches provided by their contractor provider were delicious, but Damon didn't appreciate the hot and spicy pickle relish that burned the roof of his mouth.

Someone finally asked about the bar.

"It's right there. It's open, but make sure you're ready to go with all your faculties at a moment's notice. That's a warning I don't want to have to repeat."

Two small tour busses arrived with their breakfast the next morning. They were issued local currency and shown maps of the town of Mindelo, marking the coast guard and police stations, as well as the one hospital on the island, in case of an emergency. Renny and Damon were grouped with Coop, Fredo, T.J. Talbot, and Tyler Gray. Kyle and the rest of the team were in the other van.

Their goal was to scope out each of the five sites suspected of housing what remained of the large operation that had been located at the Blue Marlin. To that end, their drivers posed as real tour operators, taking them to local bars and a couple of cathedrals for pictures. Each of the vans took a different route, and they agreed to meet up at a local tourist restaurant for lunch.

Damon's driver was from Ukraine, but he was a member of the U.S. Embassy staff. He had married a local girl he met on vacation and never left the island, except to travel to Washington for his citizenship and training. Overweight, in his fifties, and probably a heavy drinker, he showed them pictures of his young children, his "second life," as he called it.

Alexi had lots of stories, and he spoke a wicked Ukrainian-Cape Verde pigeon, or *Kreole,* as it was called.

Fredo, raised Catholic, asked about church attendance on the island. They had stopped at a quaint chapel with a stone-inlay parking lot overlooking the blue harbor. It was a favorite place to get married, he'd told them.

"Oh, we have ninety-five percent attendance here. Being from so many worlds, non-believers are considered the odd ones. We have generations of Muslim and Jewish settlers who came to escape the Inquisition. But I would say the Catholic church is the strongest."

Inside the chapel was a sacristy dedicated to war heroes, which surprised Damon.

"An honorable way to die," Alexi sighed. "And a completely wasted chance at happiness, too," he added. "Sorry, but that is my view."

"It might surprise you, but we got those too. Even some on the Teams," mumbled T.J.

"Your Kyle says all of you are lifers, yes?" Alexi asked.

That drew hearty laughter.

"We got no one and dones here," said Cooper. "As

for lifers? That's not a term I'm very familiar with. At some point, the old bod begins to break down and other shiny objects start catching our eye."

"Most of us will have knee or hip replacements before we're forty," added Damon. "Renny here is going for a brain transplant next year."

"I highly recommend that, Renny," barked T.J. "What the hell's the matter with you two? No wedding bells?"

"Fuck sake, T.J." Renny started as they piled into the van. "I'm one and done on that. And this one's fresh out of the ocean and still flopping around on deck."

Damon didn't care for the laughter taken at his expense.

"I hear he has a hook in his mouth, though," Cooper added, punching Damon in the arm.

"Afraid so. We'll be doing Facetime non-stop here." Renny would not give up.

"Does your wife like to wear skimpy underwear, and those little thongs?" asked Fredo.

"Not for you, asshole," Damon barked.

Cooper was right on that one. "Oh, Fredo has his own collection. He has a thing for lingerie. He just likes to compare."

Alexi's expression went from jovial to concerned.

"Hey, no worries, Alexi. We're just joking," soothed T.J. As he began to loosen up again, T.J. delivered the kill shot. "Fredo harkens back to his roots. Before becoming a SEAL, he was a helluva pole dancer at one of those bars in East L.A."

"Compton," Fredo corrected.

They all laughed and for the next half hour, Alexi said nothing at all. It was kind of a relief to Damon.

They traveled, through an industrial zone packed with warehouses. Driving around the side streets was extremely slow and tedious, due to the number of lorries of varying sizes picking up and making deliveries to the harbor. Since most of the island's food had to be imported, Alexi explained, large warehouses were necessary for storage. Apparently when the island was first used for inhabitants and not just farm animals, even water had to be imported, he explained.

"I'm getting a good feeling about this place. They'd have an easy time with lookouts," said T.J., who pointed out several armed men on top of the flat roofs of some of the buildings. "And they can nearly walk from one to another. No one would ever see them from down below."

Just as he said that, they watched two men leap from one building to land on their feet on another.

Alexi pointed out several more as they snaked through the bustling streets.

"I'm wondering why they'd ever take a chance and run an operation way up the hill like the Blue Marlin," asked Damon. "That seems too risky, in my opinion. They have it all here. Up there, you got one way in and one way out."

Alexi had a quick answer for that.

"For the limos, the businessmen from London, Amsterdam, Washington, D.C., my friends. It's for the floor show. You get all those dolls lined up on the balconies over there, and it's like Disneyland for perverts."

"So, they used it for staging?"

"Exactly. We locals call it the tasting room, you know, like they have for the wineries?"

"Then they could store the rest here in warehouses," whispered Renny.

"Or hold them when they offload from the ships that bring them in." He went on to explain. "The local population can't provide enough women for the trade. Besides, they have to have local cooperation. You have an expression about not shitting where you eat? Why piss off the locals, steal their women when you need their protection?"

It was making perfect sense to Damon why the operation was so successful.

"Where do they come from?" asked Tyler.

"The orient, some from Africa. You have to realize this island was developed and paid for many times over by the slave trade. The sex trafficking business is very lucrative."

Silence descended on the van.

"I know your Kyle is interested in this Freescott boy. This is the warehouse for his winery on the other side of the island."

"Winery?" asked Cooper.

"Oh yes, the Portuguese have been making wine on this island for centuries. Other than grazing cattle, it was the first agricultural endeavor here. Old families, even some pirates settled here and became huge landowners and winemakers. And Cape Verde was discovered by the Venetians for the King of Portugal, so there you go. Even your Francis Drake sailed here as a privateer."

Coop dictated addresses to T.J. who was taking copious notes.

"I like that one, and that one over there. Notice the men on top," Fredo whispered.

"Got it," answered T.J.

THEY MET UP at the Dockside cafe and tourist stop, where their van blended in well with several others from a cruise ship that had docked in the bay that morning. They took a long table and fought off a group of Italian tourists from the ship, who were jabbering like magpies and unhappy being rejected. Kyle and the rest of the Team arrived shortly thereafter.

They all ordered lobster, and beer on Alexi's recommendation.

"Don't bother with the salad. Don't order anything else that can't be frozen or stored. Fruit is excellent, though!"

Damon and Renny each ordered a half-pineapple hollowed out with a variety of local fruits that was refreshing. The lobster reminded Damon of the gulf coast in Florida.

"You guys been to one of those gulf beaches in Florida?" he asked the group.

"Outstanding!" said Kyle. "I'd like to take the kids there some day. Christy's been dying to get me committed to a trip."

"You go to one of their crab places, and you walk away—no, wait, you slide your way back to your car, you're so covered in butter," Damon added.

"What the hell are you doing out there? You're from California, Damon," asked Fredo.

Renny interrupted Damon's response. "Long story, Fredo. Don't get him started. Trust me. You don't want to hear it."

They laughed.

"I'm sorry. You did say that you are in a new relationship, Damon? Fellas, I'm wanting to hear those stories about sex on the beach and all that stuff we don't get to do any longer, right?"

"He lives vicariously through you guys," Coop explained. "He even gets turned on with Mia's soap operas.

Alexi laughed. "You should watch Ukrainian soap opera." He summed it up with, "The best ever!"

"Said no one," added Kyle.

The conversation got serious and only lasted that way for a couple of minutes.

"You all have your nominations?" Kyle asked, making eye contact with each of the Team, as they nodded. "You got your addresses and description, and your case for why, all that stuff?"

Again, everyone nodded.

"Anyone got to stop by and pick anything up on the way back?

"T.J. and I would like to see if we can pick up some Tramadol and some alcohol swabs. They sell it cheap here."

"Okay, you make sure to do that. Anybody else?"

T.J. raised his hand like a schoolboy. "I saw an advertisement for Pirate beer. I'd like to try out a case of that if we can keep it cold."

Alexi agreed. "Good local beer. Two Ukrainian fellows started it."

"Of course," T.J. said.

CHAPTER 14

PHYLLIS CLUNG TO life until the day Kaitlyn returned, never regaining consciousness.

"Not exactly the welcome home party you were hoping for. I'm so sorry, sweetie."

"They were good about updating me. Only thing I regret is that I didn't get to talk to her. I'm glad you did, though. The staff said she enjoyed your visit. Thanks, Martel."

"She called me the first day and we had a really good talk. She was so helpful. I had no idea your mother had such a sense of humor."

"Oh, there are stories. She was quite the character." Kaitlyn's voice hitched. "I go from giggling at all the things she did growing up to being really sad." She sighed. "It's a big hole to fill. But we had some great years, and she got to see Greg and I get married. I'm grateful for all that."

"I visited her when your sub told me she'd been

admitted. She was joking about getting me to rip out all the tubing and take her to the beach with an ice cream."

"Yup. That's Phyllis."

Martel's cheeks were streaked with tears. She knew Kaitlyn's probably looked the same.

"I felt a little guilty that perhaps I'd been partially responsible for getting her so worked up."

"Yeah, they told me. Don't feel that way. She probably did it on purpose. I know she couldn't have been very happy there. It all turned out the way it was supposed to."

"You're amazing, Kate."

"No, actually, I'm a little tired." She chuckled. "You probably think me a freak, but we don't do grieving in my family. She wouldn't want it that way."

"My mom was the same way when she passed."

Martel paused several minutes while a wave of sadness passed. Kaitlyn waited.

"You need help with anything? I presume you're going to take a few more days off?"

"No, I'm sticking to the schedule. I'll be missing the latter part of the school year anyway, and I need to save my sick leave."

"That's right. I forgot. And doing something you're so good at is probably the right way to spend your days now."

"That's exactly right."

"But what about her service? Can I help you with that?"

"Would you be surprised to learn she already had it all scripted and planned out? She even printed the announcements, leaving the date and times blank so all I have to do is fill them in. I would be crying, but I can hear her laughing behind me. I turn around, expecting to see her."

That part gave Martel a shiver.

SHE AND DAMON video phone conferenced nearly every day over the past week. He looked good. Being over there with his buddies seemed to buoy his mood, and some of the adventures they'd been having reminded her of how he'd been like in his early twenties. His language got filthy, however.

Renny inserted himself into their conversations often, and it annoyed her. She wanted alone time with her boyfriend, not this Boy Scout who wanted to play pranks on him. She hoped Renny wasn't getting the two of them into trouble.

She firmed the dates for the visit to Coronado and informed her landlord in Sunset Beach when she was going to return. She bought some new clothes.

Martel also made an appointment with an adoption attorney to discuss trying to locate the adoptive parents she'd placed her daughter with.

PHYLLIS' MEMORIAL SERVICE was something she never was going to forget. She'd requested to have an open casket. She had it in her will that she be dressed in a red designer suit she'd recently purchased, with matching red elbow-length gloves. The funeral home had trouble fitting the enormous red hat adorned with colorful flowers inside the casket, but they made a good try of it. Even the look of it stuffed into the box was so Phyllis.

Kaitlyn wasn't the only one who heard her mother laughing. Martel began to imagine the same thing. Especially when she took a closer look and discovered Phyllis' red gloves clutched her favorite romance novel, an especially steamy one where the hero on the cover was shirtless and wore a kilt.

Martel couldn't look Kaitlyn in the eyes for fear of bursting out laughing as she walked back to the pew. They held hands all during the service, squirming, each struggling, but not for the reasons the audience thought. Ladies from Phyllis' bridge club sat in a row behind them, and every one of them wore a flowered hat as well, as though it had been planned out in advance.

It probably was.

There was a stirring gospel song performed by a

handsome male Jamaican soloist she liked to go dancing with before she got sick. He was thirty years her junior. Several nurses from the care facility and one of her doctors attended. She even had flowers delivered by the florist she used to send to friends, and she had a big arrangement prepaid and delivered to her daughter, with tuberoses and light pink roses that had been in her wedding bouquet. She'd personalized the private note that was delivered with it.

Martel felt the strength and power of this magnificent woman reaching out to her, guiding her hand. Phyllis had never given up on life, how to live it and how to exit. Now more than ever, she wanted to take Phyllis' suggestion.

Martel knew Phyllis would be cheering her on.

ATTORNEY GRAN KARMODY had a big office on the top floor of a bank building in Tampa. Dressed in a white suit, complete with a brocade vest and gold watch, his large moustache and snow-white hair created an imposing figure on billboards, but even more so in person. He reminded her of all the images she had of a typical shrewd country lawyer, and could have been a fabulously wealthy divorce attorney.

But he had a calling. When she'd asked around for the name of an attorney to handle an adoption situation, his was always the first one on everyone's lips. He lived to place children into childless couple's homes and he fought for the birth mother and child just as if he was defending someone before the Supreme Court. It was the only kind of law he practiced.

His firm handshake nearly left a welt on the back of Martel's hand.

After she explained her situation, he didn't say a word, but remained leaning onto his desk, his hands folded before him, studying her with eyes she was sure didn't miss a thing.

"First of all, I want to say that you are a very courageous woman." His southern drawl and demeanor was charming... and just as disarming. She guessed he was probably the most formidable attorney she'd ever met.

Martel was glad that she wasn't dressed down like she had feared.

"I'm relieved," she said, placing her palm against her upper chest, swallowing.

"Well, I mean it. Now, I wouldn't normally take on a case like this. But I am moved by your story. I'm going to tell you not many women would go about this in this fashion. As a society we operate on fuzzy logic. Out of sight. Out of mind. Sometimes unwanted pregnancies are seen as inconveniences. But in my opinion, most of the women who give their child up for adoption do it because they love them. And you, little lady, are certainly one of those."

Martel was surprised. All the rehearsing in front of her bathroom mirror had paid off. She didn't want to be misunderstood and didn't want her emotions to cloud the delivery.

"Here's the problem. You signed a piece of paper"—He held up her copy of the contract—"*This* piece of paper, and it says right on it you are giving up forever your rights to any kind of claim on this child. That means even a phone call. The law is very cut and dry on this subject. They paid your expenses, and they have the right to expect what they purchased. They didn't purchase your child, Miss Long—They paid for the opportunity to be able to raise this child without any interference from you."

"And I agree with that."

"So, you can see what's happening here. Your life has changed, but you still said you would honor this contract, and that's a problem. But…"

"*They* can change their mind if I ask them."

"And that's exactly right. I'm going to recommend that you let me talk to them first. Ordinarily, when lawyers get involved it makes everyone nervous, and they should be. But in this case, they might need the kind of assurances I might be able to give them. I can tell them just what you told me. You don't want to interfere. They will forever be her parents and the people who loved and raised her. But, Miss Long, if they say no, I'm afraid I'm going to have to decline to represent you any further, because I just don't believe in undoing something as loving and unselfish as your action to give her up."

Martel's heart was beating so hard, she thought perhaps she was shaking the floor.

"Do you understand me, Miss Long?"

"I do. I completely agree."

"One other thing that bothers me a bit. This deal only goes for you. Your new beau, the father of this child, has no part in this, even though he may want to. That's a whole other can of worms. I don't want to get him started down any path where he might feel he has some rights here, because that wouldn't be fair to the parents. Assuming your child is happy, they are reasonable people, AND you are respectful of their position, they may include him at some future date, but I'm not going to even bring it up. We don't need that kind of complication. Are you okay with that?"

"I am." She hesitated to ask him her next question. "What are my chances?"

"You met them back then. I'm guessing your meeting was amicable, and you've lived up to your part of the bargain. We'll just have to see what's in their hearts. I really can't predict, Miss Long. But I promise I'll argue your request with all the delicacy and respect I can muster. And if they say no, I'll make sure to leave the door open and let them know, if they change their mind, I'll always be here. Now, is all that acceptable?"

"Thank you, Mr. Karmody," she said as she stood.

"You got it, ma'am. My pleasure."

MARTEL WALKED OUT of the office arm-in-arm with the spirit of Phyllis Carrington. She even bought an ice cream on the way home.

CHAPTER 15

THE TEAM MADE a schedule of the couriers, the deliveries and police that frequented the two buildings identified as most likely to be working the illegal network. After days of night surveillance, Kyle was confident several of the other targets could in fact be decoys, or places where things could be quickly stashed if an operation went against the cartel's interest.

During the day, those buildings were generally not guarded.

Damon, Renny, Coop and Fredo were assigned to break in, and verify this. And they had to do it in the middle of the day, without causing attention.

The team wasn't heavily armed. Fredo did carry his usual supply of flash bombs and explosive caps, but everyone else brought only their designated sidearm. In Damon's case, it was his SigSauer. Coop carried a medic bag, and Fredo was responsible for communicating with Kyle.

Armando and Danny had quietly broken into adjacent buildings to set up cover from the roof. One factory manufactured tee shirts, dresses, and other textiles for the tourist trade. The other was a packing and shipping operation. They'd been selected because of a series of external fire escapes, leading inside without detection. They signaled they were in place and Fredo gave the green light.

The four others split up, each attempting to break in from opposite sides of their targeted buildings. Damon and Renny made it inside and noticed Fredo, who managed to jimmy a sliding metal door that had come off its track. They peered through the furniture, boxes and household goods stored in clusters around the ground floor. There were catwalks and tiny offices upstairs, but no real second floor. Under a tarp in the corner, a brand-new police vehicle was stored.

Renny was in charge of taking pictures with the specialized phone, for uploading back home. Kyle gave the go-ahead to check out the offices upstairs. The team found them all completely vacant.

Damon verified all clear in the rear alleyway while Fredo and Coop attempted to leave the broken cargo bay in the same condition as they'd found it. The other door was left locked.

While Danny and Armando repositioned themselves, the four men loitered nearby, slowly working their way to the other building they needed to investigate.

Given the all-clear, Damon and Renny couldn't get the deadbolt open on the heavy metal door facing the narrow alleyway at the rear. They found an open window instead and crawled through. Fredo and Coop joined them. The four entered a small office, set up with a telephone, a copy machine, and a cot with pillow and folded blankets. The door leading to the warehouse portion locked from the inside. Fredo opened it a crack, and bright light shone through, nearly blinding them. Music played in the distance.

The warehouse was not vacant but very much in use. Bright hanging fluorescent lights illuminated the huge space, revealing shipping boxes and wooden crates stacked over one story tall. Tables were laid out in lines, end to end. Piles of books sat at various places at the tables. A variety of mismatched chairs were placed along the lines for seating. A big screen T.V. hung from the wall. Two leather couches sat facing each other with a small trunk being used as a coffee table between them.

But there wasn't any evidence of anyone working there.

Finally, a door opened. The sound of music got louder, and then they heard the remnants of a toilet flush as a male worker brought out his portable radio, set it on one of the tables, and sat with his back to them. He began boxing books in cardboard mailers.

Coop motioned for Renny to take pictures before they closed the door and checked in with Kyle.

"Check to see if the phone line is live," Damon could hear Kyle's squawk over Fredo's mic. He picked up the receiver and heard a dial tone, nodded, which was then relayed to Kyle.

Coop broke into a locked file cabinet and perused files inside, holding his flashlight in his mouth. He pulled out a letter and a couple other items, folded them, and tucked them into his vest.

Damon located an untaped box of books ready to ship out. Inside were illustrated children's bible stories, written in Portuguese. He held one up, and Coop directed him to tuck it in his medic backpack.

"We're done here," whispered Fredo. "Moving out.

ALL SIX OF them returned with their goods to the Blue Marlin.

"Wish we could have had a look upstairs in that building, so let's assume they sometimes have a crew sleeping over, just to be safe," Kyle said.

"So, are we good to go tonight then?" asked Coop.

"I think that's everything we need. I agree, the wine storage facility is where we'll likely find the girls and hopefully Samantha."

He gave instructions on who were on the two teams. Armando and Danny would first get into position to cover them from adjacent rooftops Armando had already picked out. The remaining ten would split into two teams and would break in, hopefully with the element of surprise.

No one had seen Samantha Raymond during their many surveillance forays, but several other women with armed male escorts were seen entering the building only at night. During the day, two shooters were camped out on top of both buildings, frequently changing locations. And, they were wired. But at night, for some reason, the rooflines were left unguarded.

"Get a power nap. No distractions or calling home. We got to be focused. Make sure you bring everything with you in case we don't come back here, as nice as it is. Check your weapons, your tools of the trade, gents. We roll at midnight. It's a new moon, so the odds are in our favor."

Kyle's instructions were simple, and easy to follow. It was the unknown that always fucked with them, Damon thought to himself. He crashed hard as soon as his head hit the pillow.

ON THE WAY to the site, Renny offered Damon some bubble gum. His mouth was parched, and he noted he hadn't been hydrating enough. Of course, the salty food they'd been eating, especially the locally prepared fish dishes, didn't help.

Alexi and the other driver waited nervously while the Team took what they needed and left the rest, heading to the two buildings.

Armando and Danny signaled they were in place and the roof was secure. Kyle gave the all clear for the rest of the team to get into position. It had been determined that no deliveries happened at night until early in the morning at 0600. That's when trucks would be arriving to start loading freight, occasionally with an armed guard contingent in a Jeep or Rover of some kind. Their goal was to strike before any of the increased manpower arrived. The two breaches had to be timed perfectly.

An abandoned chair sat outside the rear entrance, illuminated by a single bulb fixture.

"Danny, can you kill the light?" Damon heard Kyle ask.

A second later, they heard the ping of a rock and then the tinkle of glass as Danny's slingshot removed the problem. They waited to see if anyone took notice, and after five minutes, continued with the plan.

The other building was lit with a large high-pressure sodium vapor light mounted tall that would have to be shot out during the breach. They were ready. Kyle made the decision not to use their NV goggles because they expected someone would throw the lights on.

Fredo first checked the door, and found it locked. He applied the explosive charge, while Coop rigged up the other building. With Armando and Danny ready— and the charges placed, Kyle gave the go.

The blast tore the metal door off its hinges. Amongst the screams from what sounded like women, Fredo, Damon, Renny, and the others on their squad entered and quickly fanned out to the sides, their backs against the wall. It was pitch black until someone flipped the switch and the room lit up like Christmas. Fredo threw some smoke to help as the team looked for guards they expected would be present.

Women and children ran back and forth in their night clothes through the smoke, looking for a safe place to hide. Two shooters started firing down on the SEALs. Jameson and Tucker quickly took them out.

Damon tripped over a cot, which turned out to be lucky as he heard a round hit the concrete floor where he'd been standing. Before he could fully turn around, T.J. fired, hitting the shooter in the head. He tossed the MP5 over to Jameson, who would be their designated indoor sharpshooter, along with some clips.

As Jameson focused on picking off men pouring out from several upstairs rooms, Damon and Renny counted the women and children, looking for Samantha. He called for Cooper when he found one of the girls had gotten caught in the crossfire and had taken a round to the upper thigh that was bleeding out dangerously. The nimble medic quickly applied a tourniquet while Damon covered him and continued sorting the women.

Renny's scream pierced the air.

"Go. I'm good," yelled Coop. He pulled the young girl to the side and deposited her in the huddle of other prisoners.

Damon found Renny on the ground, but alive. He'd been stabbed in the chest and somehow the blade had sliced under his armor. It was still protruding, the pearl handle covered in bloody fingerprints.

T.J. nodded to another interior doorway, directing Damon to take out a man talking on a hand-held radio. Without any hesitation, he flew at the young guard, twisting his neck and sending him to the floor in a heap. When he opened the door, he spotted Samantha scampering to hide herself in the closet of a makeshift bedroom.

"Sam? That you?" Damon asked.

She slowly poked her head out between the clothes. Damon saw movement on his right and quickly disabled the young man holding a large machete over his head. The man's arm was clearly broken, but

Damon went down on his knees to break the guy's neck when Samantha screamed, "No!"

That's when he realized the boy was Kwanda Freescott's son.

Tucker burst into the room and helped Damon remove Samantha and Mr. Freescott after securing his wrists in a zip tie. The painful process had the young man screaming as Samantha fought to be at his side.

Damon held her by her hair. "I'm going to tie you up just like him if you don't cooperate. We're here to rescue, not assassinate. We're taking you home."

"I don't want to go home!" she screamed.

Damon shoved her on the bed and zip tied her wrists, pushing her out of the room behind her lover. The building had become eerily calm, except for the moaning and crying of the huddled women and children.

Fredo rushed over, eyeing the two captives. "Kyle wants to know how many."

"I counted twenty-two, plus these two."

Fredo relayed the message and came back with instructions. "We take them with us. He's leading another seventeen over, and they'll be turned over to the locals. We take these two back with us."

The other driver agreed to wait for the police, while Alexi drove them to the harbor. He tossed the Freescott kid to the side and took up a seat next to Renny. T.J.

gave him a wink and nod, indicating he was free to mess with his buddy to keep his mood light until they got some medical attention.

"Just another day in paradise, right?"

"Fuck you, Damon. I see you went for the girl while I took the blade."

"Yeah, I got the cushy job, didn't I?"

He saw Kyle smile and lean against a window as the van bounced around, eventually coming to a two-lane freeway with a sign showing a boat, water and an arrow.

"See that? We're going on a little fishing trip, Renny."

His friend's eyes got wide. "I'm not standing anywhere near you, Damon."

Now that would be funny, puking all over the Team.

With all the adrenaline coursing through his system, he figured it was the same as consuming a full bottle of Dramamine.

But it still would be funny.

CHAPTER 16

MARTEL ANXIOUSLY WATCHED the ground rise up to meet the plane's landing gear. It had been three months since she'd seen Damon, though they talked frequently on video chat. When she learned about Renny, she didn't even mind that occasionally he'd pop up on the screen, his chest still wrapped in white bandages.

She'd had lots of time to think about what might or might not happen this trip. It needed to be more than just a good time. If they were going to take their relationship to the next level, which meant revealing her decision of ten years ago, it had to be something she was certain of. What Damon was asking was for her to see herself living with him in California. Taking her from the roots she'd planted in Florida, tearing her away from the beautiful sunsets and the white beach. Nothing in California could ever match that.

But she would give it an honest try. She guarded

her expectations. She was looking for real this time.

Damon met her at the luggage turnstile. He'd let his stubble grow, and it roughed him up and gave him an even more masculine, older look she liked.

"Hey, babe. I've missed you so much," he whispered as they embraced. He carefully placed a long kiss on her lips in full view of the entire planeload of passengers. She could tell her cheeks had pinked up.

"Me too. Merry almost Christmas!"

"I'm not thinking Christmas at all. I'm so distracted with you being here, it could be Valentine's or Fourth of July."

She wrinkled her nose. "Valentine's is fun. I like that one."

"Oh, you do, do you?" he answered, his hand smoothing over her butt and making her jump.

"You're ruining my reputation," she whispered.

"Oh, they know. Look at them," he said as he caught several people watching them. "They know what you're all about."

He picked up her bag, and they walked through the lobby to the short-term parking lot. Damon opened the passenger door of his brand new bright blue Hummer, and helped her up the step to inside the cab.

"You went shopping."

"I didn't want to ferry you around in my Jasmine."

Jasmine had been the name of his old Ford pick-up

he'd owned ten years ago. "You still had her? You mean you left her out to pasture?"

He smiled and closed the door. He tucked her suitcase into the second seat. Once behind the steering wheel, he explained.

"Jasmine was costing me a small fortune to keep her tuned up and working reliably. She was letting me down a bunch. So she's now happy, getting greasy with all those old crusty guys at the wrecking yard. She was a classic, but after we got back, I decided I'd reward myself with a new set of wheels. Meet Monica."

They drove down along the waterfront district, past several cruise ships in port, and several military floating museums, including the USS Midway. Tall silvery structures overlooked a packed marina filled with expensive yachts. They passed the Convention Center and continued South and then across the Coronado Bridge to the strand.

"Are you tired or are you up for a burger and a brew?"

"I want to see some place where you hang out. Some place, that Scupper, is that it? Is that nearby?"

"Yes, ma'am."

She noticed the sun had set some time ago, but the orange glow didn't stain the sky as long as it did in Florida. But the weather was nice, even in the middle of December.

"You're looking for the sunset, aren't you?"

"I've gotten accustomed to it."

"They're nice here, but Florida's warmer, when it doesn't hurricane."

Walking through the doors at the Scupper, she studied the artwork covering the walls, pictures of Team guys and sailors, photos of various ships, flags from different campaigns, and copies of telegrams and letters from Presidents. One entire wall contained pictures of young men who had not been able to come home. It was very sobering. Damon watched her carefully.

They were seated outside on the patio, next to a fire pit.

Everything she saw was unfamiliar. It was busier and larger than her sleepy little Sunset Beach town. The cars were more expensive and the streets were teeming with groups of handsome muscled men and young women out having a good time. She could feel right away it was a faster pace, like how Sonoma County had felt when she returned there after living in Oregon for the year on the coast and for her college.

He kept watching her.

"What do you think?"

"It suits you, I can see. You're happy here, aren't you, Damon?"

He nodded and sipped on his beer. "Very."

She raised her glass and toasted him. "That's why I like it."

THE TOUCH OF his hands on her body was like heaven. She even felt slightly embarrassed standing naked against him in the shower. He soaped all the airport and Florida dust from her skin, massaged the back of her neck until she relaxed and became putty in his arms again. It didn't take long. He was patient.

Their fooling around in the shower spilled over to the bedroom, where at last they lay together, wet but warmed by the sensual shower. He pulled the comforter over them, making a tent. She felt the creases at the sides of his mouth, the way his ears felt like velvet, the smell of his chest even though she'd soaped him off and rinsed him with her bare hands. His whispers drew out all her animal spirits until at last he touched her like it was the first time.

As she peaked, her orgasm taking over her body, she held him as tightly as she was able. She needed to feel him deep and to experience how well they fit together and how she never wanted to let him go.

Her life was full, surrounded by strong women from her past, and a mission and fire in her soul. She was living the life, holding the man in her arms that few women had the good fortune to love. He was fearless, and through that, everything was possible.

For now, she tossed aside her worries as well as her plans and just enjoyed the way he coveted her and turned that night into magic.

HE TOOK HER to breakfast at a restaurant beside the Convention Center, where they meandered down the pier, eyeing expensive yachts from all over the world.

"I came here the morning after I went skydiving for the first time," he said. "I was scared shitless, and after doing that, I just wanted to stock up on carbs big time. I felt as strong as a Sherman tank, and as light as a feather!"

"If that is your way of asking if I'd like to jump out of a plane, I have to tell you that I'm an earth person. I do gardens, enjoy roadtrips, and love beaches and beautiful blue water. But floating through the sky? I don't think I could ever do that."

"Would you trust me to go tandem?"

"Not sure what that means."

"I strap on behind you, I tell you what to do, and we fly together. You'd love it."

"Damon, you're crazy. I'd never do that."

"Sure you would. I know you have it in you. Don't you want to find out?" He held her hand. "I'd be right there with you the whole way, strapped to your back."

SHE KNEW THAT if he waited until tomorrow or the

next day she'd chicken out. Before she knew it, they were at the glider center, watching one plane after another load up, take off and then allow their passengers to slowly float back down to the ground. Except for the idea of seeing houses that appeared one-half inch wide, the process didn't look scary at all.

They were fitted with tandem chutes. A short instruction class began, telling her how her chute would open, what she would see, how to land, and how to position her arms and angle her body for the maximum good experience.

And then they were off in the airplane that didn't have a door on the large opening she watched in front of her as they climbed to over thirteen thousand feet. The cars and trucks were the size of chocolate sprinkles on the doughnut she ate this morning. Panic was setting in. She considered asking Damon to take her back to the base.

"Stand up, sweetheart," he whispered and kissed the side of her cheek.

She did so, and he hooked himself to her harness, and they walked to the opening like one crab-like being. "When do we…"

Damon nudged her into the opening and over the edge. The freefall she experienced wasn't what she expected. Instead of falling, she was being pushed up by air coming from the earth.

He reminded her to keep her mouth closed because she'd been screaming. He touched her arms and she assumed the "W" position she'd been shown.

"Lean forward, legs back. Now pull this."

All of a sudden, the chute unfurled into a beautiful red and yellow kite flying overhead. Objects on the ground were still very small, but the closer they got to earth, the warmer the air got. They could talk because the wind had stopped screaming all around her.

"See? Not so bad now, right?"

"It's beautiful."

"There's Mexico over there." He started pointing out ships and buildings they'd passed, including the harbor and the Convention Center. "There's my Hummer, see it?"

Now his truck looked the size of her little fingernail.

He showed her how to pull on the weighted steering, making them turn, first to the right, and then to the left, hitting thermals which sent them back up small distances. It was peaceful and kissed with glorious sunlight. And she was with him.

She held his hand as he steered the glider expertly, prolonging their descent. And as they got close to the ground, he asked her to shoot her feet out in front, while they landed on his, and then they tumbled in the grasses and stopped.

On her back, tethered in the straps of her chute, her arms out to the sides, she looked up at the sky, blue and overwhelming, and felt the magic and the power of being alive.

He was there, watching her, kissing her gently, and witnessing the miracle together. She trusted him. She trusted herself not to let fear hold her back.

She embraced her future, whatever that was to be.

THE NEXT MORNING, she received the call from Gran Karmody. The Newbergs wanted to meet with her and discuss her request.

Martel knew that her past had finally come back to greet her. Would she be risking this beautiful love story for the chance to meet her daughter? She felt like she was stepping through another doorway to the freefall, except this time, she wasn't strapped into safety.

It would be completely uncharted waters.

And it would be worth it.

CHAPTER 17

DAMON WATCHED MARTEL chatting with several of the SEAL wives at the Team 3 Christmas party, held at the Brownlee home. As was usual, the Brownlee's tree filled the nearly two-story Spanish Renaissance home in one of the most exclusive areas of Coronado. Many of the SEAL children, if they were old enough to remember, were excited to find their little gifts the Brownlees placed under the tree. A crowd of nearly a dozen, including some toddlers who were shoved aside by the older children, had to be reminded to be careful not to disturb the tree or the ornaments.

Martel laughed at their antics, trying to follow the action while turning back to stay involved in the conversation with the wives and girlfriends.

Dr. and Mrs. Brownlee were Libby's parents, Coop's in-laws. A noted psychiatrist and frequent talk show guest as well as bestselling author, Dr. Brownlee had become the Team unofficial shrink, in all ways but legally. His own brother, Will, had been a Navy SEAL medic who perished in Grenada. As was tradition, his name was engraved on the ceremonial KA-BAR knife presented to Coop when he got his Trident. Kyle had ordered him to find out about the family of this fallen Bonefrog, since Coop had just lost all of his in a tornado in his home state of Nebraska.

And that's where he'd met his wife, Libby, who was Will Brownlee's niece.

The party was packed this year. Sometimes, the Team was deployed overseas, and only the wives and children were present. Or some of them would be on temporary assignments or extra training duties. But this year, it was nearly a full house. Luckily, the weather was nice enough that tables were spread outside around the huge Brownlee pool and patio area.

"That sure didn't take you long," whispered Cooper. He was joined by T.J. in admiring his choice.

Damon didn't mind the implied dig. His divorce had just been finalized since he hadn't contested anything and let Charlene keep the house.

"Funny how the right woman comes along at just the right time," he said as he smiled in her direction. Then he faced Coop and T.J. "We were sweethearts ten years ago, just before I got out of Dodge and signed up. I'm lucky she seems to like having me back," he said.

"I'll bet. Night and day between her and the other

one," T.J. mumbled.

"She who will remain unnamed," added Coop.

"May she rot in Hell and choke on the house payments," said Damon.

"Glad that's all settled then." Coop sipped on his mineral water. "So, have you asked her yet?"

Damon squinted and sucked in air through his teeth. "We're not quite there. Close. But not quite there. Lots of implied consent, if you know what I mean."

"Oh, sweetheart, I love you. I never want to be without you!" T.J. mimicked, pumping his hips.

Damon still didn't take offense. "Not like that at all," he shook his head. "We're taking it slow and steady. We're exploring all sorts of options. Just getting to know each other again after such a long time apart."

"I myself like it slow and hard," mumbled T.J.

"The exploring part sounds kind of fun to me. You use handcuffs and strawberry gel and the titty cream?" asked Coop.

Damon did begin to get rattled at that comment. "How come you fellas never talked about this before with me?"

"Because you were a married man. Miserable, but married, Damon," answered T.J.

"We live vicariously through all of you divorced or single guys. We like hearing about new love and wicked sex. Sometimes being long-term married with a couple of kids running around begins to get a bit routine, if you know what I mean," added Coop.

"But that's what I want."

The two SEALs stared at Damon incredulously.

Damon couldn't hold it more than ten seconds. His smile cracked, and soon they all were laughing. As they wandered off in search of another victim, T.J. punched him in the arm. "Good one. You're all right. I was worried about you for a while."

ON THE WAY back to Damon's place, he asked her how she felt being at the party.

"Lovely ladies. And those kids, they're bright, mostly polite, but Danny's got a little hellion."

"Oh, that's Ali. He rescued him from Iraq and adopted him. I think he was about three or four and had been living in a war zone. All his family was killed. His father died trying to save him."

"That's an amazing story."

"He's deadly accurate with a slingshot. Danny taught him and usually, his little brother, Griffin, has a bruise on his forehead. Griffin is his favorite target."

"That's terrible."

"He's been sent home from school dozens of times. They've got their hands full."

"Luci is lovely. She's got the patience of Job with

three boys."

"So you didn't really answer my question."

"I can see why you love working with these guys and their families. I understand now. I never did before. But you all are a big family."

"Something goes wrong, we're there for each other. The wives too. Only thing we aren't supposed to do is gossip, but it happens sometimes. Sometimes the wives don't get it, start moving out of the circle, and that just does not work here. We stick together."

"I can see that." Martel continued to stare through the windshield, and sighed.

Damon wondered if he'd come on too strong. But he needed to know there was no resistance on her part. His goal was to get her to commit, agree to move out to California as soon as she could arrange it. He was ready to lay down roots and make up for lost time.

But she was being a little elusive.

"What's wrong?"

She turned. "Nothing. Why would you think that?"

He shrugged. "I don't know. You just seem…preoccupied."

"Well, it's all new, Damon. I grew up in California, but I spent most of that up north, as you know. A world apart from Southern California. And nothing like Florida."

"I didn't have to spend much time getting adjusted

there," he chuckled.

"It's really not the same thing, Damon. In Florida, things are slower. You take off your uniform, your big boots, put on your shorts and flip flops. You hang out on the patio and watch the sun set every night. You eat seafood and dance at moonlight."

She meant it. Life was harder for her in San Diego.

"Would you miss it?" He focused on his driving so she didn't feel pressured.

"I'm learning to adjust. I could probably learn to adjust anywhere if you were there, Damon. And I like the Damon I fool around with here. I like his shower, his bed, his aftershave. I even like the way he drives his new truck."

"Hummer."

"It's a truck."

"No, it's a Hummer. Big difference." He pulled over and turned off the engine. They weren't home, but near a little park overlooking the ocean. A large gray cruiser glided past them on its way back to the base. "Come on," he said as he pulled her over the gear shift and out through the driver's door.

Martel was laughing, pretending to try to get away. With her hair blowing in the gentle breeze and the water as a backdrop behind her, Damon fell to his knees.

"I'm crazy about you. I don't need any more time

trying to figure it out. I want you here. I'm all done with my search. You're the one, Martel. Please tell me you'll marry me."

He could see a cloud form in her eyes. It wasn't the pure love and acceptance he'd expected. Was she going to say no?

She slowly knelt down in front of him and took his hands in hers. "Just give me a little time. I want the same thing, Damon. I move a little slower. Remember, I'm working on Florida time."

He tried not to show his disappointment. He'd been totally convinced she would be delighted, and they'd be making their rounds tonight, telling everyone they were engaged. What had happened?

"Damon," she started, "Think of it this way. A good couple who are going to spend the rest of their lives together is a blending of two people. They are not the same. You're the guy who loves doing things that are wild and active. I read, and yes, I enjoy learning about all the things you do, but my world is one of books— and teaching children to read. And maybe it takes longer for my brain and my heart to get in sync. It's not a bad thing that we approach life differently. We can't all be heroes and save the day. And you wouldn't want that, either."

He could see she'd spent a lot of time thinking about it, which bothered him further. He was torn between asking for explanation and considering that it would be best to let her figure it out on her own. He wouldn't be able to convince her. She had to get there on her own. And that's why she was here.

She wouldn't have come if she wasn't considering spending the rest of her life with me.

Their hands were still clutched together. She reached over and touched his cheek. "Damon, sweetheart, I want this to work. I really do. I'm sorting, processing, letting pieces fall into place. That's what works for me."

"You're right." He had to cut off the discussion. Perhaps he'd scared her or started out wrong.

They held hands back to the truck, and he helped her in again. Before he closed her door, he leaned in. "You just let me know if you have questions I need to answer. I'm going to let you do the sorting out, like you said. I trust you, Martel. We have no secrets, right? There isn't anything or anyone standing in the way? I just want to be sure."

Her eyes watered. She touched his cheek again. "No."

But she was still crying when he pulled up to his place. And she couldn't tell him what movie she wanted to go to tonight, since that had been the plan. He suggested they rent one, and she was agreeable, but didn't have any preferences.

He knew he could make love to her, perhaps brighten her mood, caress, and work out all the second thoughts or worry she must be harboring. But he sort of didn't want to do that tonight.

"It's a lot to take in here, I know. Why don't you take a shower and go to bed early? I'm going to stay up and watch a little T.V. Then I'll come and join you," he said, giving her a short kiss.

She didn't pull him to her. She didn't do anything at all except nod, look at her feet, and slip away into the bedroom, closing the door behind her.

He sat for several minutes in the dark and stared at that door. He didn't know what was on the other side, but it wasn't anything he could fight or manipulate. He had to wait. That was the most fucked up thing in the world right now.

PAST MIDNIGHT, DAMON awoke with a kink in his neck from falling asleep upright on the couch. He'd been tired. Kind of a nervous energy, he thought.

Opening the door slowly to stop any noise, he tiptoed inside the bedroom, removed his shoes and clothes, and slipped into the sheets in his boxers. Her warm body had heated up the bed, and he became aroused, in spite of his decision to pull back a bit on his expectation and emotions.

But he felt her hand travel over his chest and up his

neck. He accepted the gift of her soft body as it touched his, her thigh over his, her breasts rubbing against him, and the moan she gave him as their lips touched. She pulled her hair back and continued to kiss his neck and down the center of his chest. Her right hand smoothed over his thigh, lacing her fingers up and then down as they traveled toward his package. She arched up and placed him between her breasts and squeezed their flesh together.

His hardness was instantaneous as she undulated over him, gently riding his thigh, letting him feel her mound pressed firmly against him. She spread her legs wide, held onto him with both hands, massaged him up and down, and then touched his tip with her tongue, rubbing and probing. She gently sucked as he breached her lips, her tongue wrapping around him.

She kissed him from stem to his tip—then squeezed and fondled his balls. Her breathing became deep, the pressure increased until he couldn't be still any longer. He sat up, partially, framing her face with his hands.

"That's so nice, sweetheart."

She drew him in deep, all the way to the back of her throat and held him.

He was about to burst. He needed to get inside her, but she was insistent, working up and down on his shaft, increasing his size, turning him into a Grecian column.

He slid up the bed and she followed. Leaning against the padded headboard, he watched as her long hair framed her face, as she climbed up first one thigh and then the other. She gently rubbed him back and forth against her pulsing sex. She braced herself, holding on to the headboard with both hands while she angled her hips and let him seat completely inside her.

Damon gasped when her muscles enclosed him, as he felt the warm friction of the insides of her channel. He brought his hands to her breasts. Moving his hips, he forced himself deep inside her. She leaned over, presenting her nipples to his mouth and he sucked them into peaks. He pushed up and inside, back and forth until the movement became faster and faster. His thighs slapped against hers, his cock gliding quickly through the gateway of her sex. Until she arched up and moaned. Her insides fluttered.

He grabbed her ass, gripped her hips, and quickly flipped her over to fuck her deep from behind as she came. The satisfying constriction of his balls, responding to the new position, sent him spurting inside her. He held her tight against him, pushing as she pressed back against him. She found his hands and added pressure, followed his fingers as they tweaked her bud.

And then they stopped, breathing, waiting for the pulsing to stop, prolonging the moment for as long as they could.

The next morning, she was back. She matched every advance he made. She walked around in her robe untied, teasing him with her nakedness. They spent the next two days in bed. All the things they needed to do were put onto the backburner as he explored how deep and long he could feel consumed by this woman. He was going to give her every ounce she demanded. He'd be relentless. The two of them together would not be like Coop and T.J. Their only routine was feeling more, getting deeper and making the addiction last forever.

This was the way he was supposed to live.

SHE WAS TO return home in three days. She told him she'd extended her stay by two because she'd run across an old friend from Oregon, who was now living in the Bay Area.

"Great. We'll take a road trip!" He was all for it.

She stood against him, touching his lips with her forefinger. "Damon, I need to meet with her alone."

"Sure. I'll drive. You have your meeting, and we'll do some fun stuff, and then return. It'll be a great trip."

Her eyes studied him. "This is important. This is something I need to do by myself."

"What do you mean?"

"I want to just fly up there on my own. They're living in Palo Alto now. I haven't seen them in ten years."

"Them?"

"She's married. We have some history. I needed to clear the air with her at first. Later, perhaps another visit, we can all be together, but not for this first meeting, Damon."

He broke away, sitting on the couch. He didn't like what he was hearing.

"You've never mentioned this friend. What sort of friend are we talking about, Martel? A lover?"

"No, please. I'll tell you all about it after the meeting. I promise. I just need you to trust me."

"But we decided not to have any secrets. And now you've got one. I'm not part of that."

"It isn't like that. Believe me, this is different. I'm going to tell you the whole story, soon. I'll be safe. I've made a promise to myself, to her, to my mother. I'm promising you I have to do this initially by myself. I just can't talk about it further."

He stiffened.

"This is really strange, Martel. What the hell is this all about?"

"Something that happened when I was in school up in Oregon. It's not bad—"

"Then tell me!"

"I promise I will. I'm just not ready yet."

So that was it. She had some big fucking secret he wasn't included in. Was this some former colleague, a lover? Did she have an affair with a woman? Is that what she was afraid to tell him?

He wanted to ask but didn't want her to be offended in case he was wrong. He decided to go for it anyway. "Look, Martel, if this woman is someone you were romantically involved with, I don't care. As long as you're not asking me to share you with her husband, or share me with her, I'm fine with something from your past that meant something to you. I wasn't there. But now that I'm here, I really beg you to let me be a part of it."

"You will be, Damon. I promise. It isn't fair to ask you, but I must ask that you trust me."

So, THERE IT was.

She took all her things, and he even dropped her off at the airport the next day. Her friend, she said, was going to meet her in San Francisco.

"I'll text you so you know I've gotten there safely," she'd said.

"Fine. Can I ask one more question before you go?"

"Of course."

"Are you coming back?"

The look on her face broke his heart. As he watched her cross the concourse toward the gates, he wondered if it would be the last time he'd ever see her.

He wanted to feel something, but he was in shock.

Maybe he was dead and had just figured it out, like in the movie.

This was friendly fire. The worst kind.

CHAPTER 18

E VERY TIME MARTEL felt the cramp in her stomach and her shortness of breath, she put it out of her mind. Someone had told her that the Special Forces operators did a good job of masking pain, even being able to stop bleeding in a critical situation, if they were trained properly.

She was far from having that skill. But distraction was helping.

The bay wasn't anything like Tampa Bay, where the water was so delineated people could live along the edge. These edges curled around like some alien oil painting. Parts of the bay were purple, part dark brown. It reminded her of her trip to Yellowstone when she was a child and viewing all the little steamy mud pools of different colors.

When the wheels touched the ground, she was shaken to reality. Lori Newberg was going to meet her at the luggage carousel. Although she'd seen the woman years ago, she wasn't sure she'd recognize her.

As she descended down the escalator, the Newbergs stood together, arm in arm, a safe distance from the limo drivers who were picking up their charges. Lori's hair was shorter now, and had turned salt-and-pepper gray. She wore a red long-sleeved wool dress with a hooded rain parka in a light tan color. Mark wore a long black raincoat over his suit trousers. He'd worn a white shirt and red tie. His horn-rimmed glasses pegged him as a professor at Stanford or a school administrator. Neither of them smiled. In fact, Martel saw Lori tighten her grip on her husband's arm and seem to draw strength from him.

She'd rehearsed what she would say to the couple, and now everything she'd practiced went out the window. When she noticed Lori's eyes were watering, Martel knew what to do.

"First, let me say I'm grateful. Very grateful for what you've done and also for giving me the opportunity to speak with you both. I hesitated for so long—"

Mark pointed to the moving turnstile. "What color? I'll get your suitcase."

"It's big and brown with a turtle design on it. I bought it in Hawaii."

As Mark ran off to get the bag, Lori cleared her throat. She inhaled. "Well. Here we are again. I wasn't sure how I'd feel about all this."

"Me too." Martel smiled at her. She could see the woman was stressed, as she would be.

"God, did you bring sand from Florida?" he said struggling to get the handle pulled.

"Oh, I didn't tell you, I've been visiting friends in San Diego. I've been in California over a week now."

"Christmas break for you too, right?" Lori asked as they made their way out of the baggage area and into the parking lot. A light rain was falling.

"Yes." She was going to tell them about her new boyfriend but decided not to do so. "And in case you're worrying I brought such a big bag, I'm only staying until tomorrow and then I fly home—I mean I fly back to San Diego and then back to Florida in another four days."

"You said you got a room in Palo Alto?" Mark asked. "Where is your reservation?"

"The Stanford Court. Thought I might go do some last-minute Christmas shopping too." Her attempts at being light-hearted were not working. Not only wasn't she relaxing them, but she was making herself nervous as hell. She started noticing everything she didn't like about her wardrobe, starting with the new loafers she'd bought that were giving her blisters. She wasn't used to wearing long pants and wool, multi-layers and sweaters, even in the middle of December.

"Stanford Court is nice, and it's not far from our

house, is it, Mark?" Lori asked.

"Yup."

As Mark opened the car doors for both her and Lori, she thanked them both for picking her up at the airport.

"No problem. We're glad to," Mark said.

No one said anything on the way to Palo Alto from the airport. Afternoon traffic was beginning to congest the freeway. She used the time to send a text to Damon, which wasn't read. She added another line, asking what he wanted her to get for his late Christmas present.

Martel checked in, giving the bellman ten dollars to bring the bag up to her room.

She'd already called ahead and knew that they had a bar area and coffee shop off the lobby that wouldn't be very crowded that time of day.

"Should we sit in here?" she motioned to the tables. Two big screen T.V.'s were playing sports, but the volume was mercifully turned low. She let them select the table. Mark ordered a Scotch, but Lori and Martel both had water.

Mark leaned into the table, his brow furled. "I have to air something first, if you don't mind. Are we going to be sued?"

"Oh heck no! Why—oh you thought since Mr. Karmody contacted you that I had those intentions. I don't."

"Well, that's what he said too. I feel I should tell you that Lori and I are not rich, but we'll spend every penny we have trying to defend our right to keep Ainsley. We have several friends who are well-connected here in Silicon Valley who said they'd help. I'm not here to fight—"

"Nor am I," Martel interrupted him. "Honest. I'm not here to interfere with your rights as her parents, her *real* parents. I'm just here to make my request. Just once, I'd like to talk to her, to have her hear it from me that I didn't abandon her, that I arranged it so you could have her, and raise her the way I couldn't. But I didn't abandon her." Martel feared the last part. "I did it for love, because I love her."

Lori's eyes were spilling over her lower lids now. "Why do you have to do that? Whatever gives you the right?"

Martel looked between the two wonderful people who were lucky enough to have her little girl. It was strange sitting across the table from them and feeling grateful for what they'd done. She wished she could make them see that.

She took Lori's hand. "Because I wanted her to know that she was and is loved. That she wasn't discarded. She's always been loved."

Lori withdrew her hand and blotted her eyes with the napkin. "We've told her that many, many times."

"I know that. But I want her to hear it from me."

Mark was concerned for Lori, and it was obvious he was going to support her in any way she wanted. He waited until her composure came back.

"Why should I trust you?"

"Because I only held her for a few minutes. I just wanted her to know what was in my heart when I let her go."

Lori looked into her lap. She extracted a picture of a preteen girl, tall and lanky, blonde, wearing a basketball uniform, holding a ball in her hands. She was the spitting image of her father.

Martel didn't want to touch the photo but stared down at her daughter, seeing the shape of her face, the way her button nose flared out to the sides but had a flat spot, just like hers. When she held her in the hospital, she'd noticed all those things. She'd kissed her forehead, and handed her to the nurse.

Something distracted her on her blouse, and Martel noticed she'd been crying.

"She's beautiful, Lori. She's even prettier than I imagined."

Mark spoke up. "She's a helluva basketball player. She's good at every kind of sport we can find her. She plays soccer, baseball, basketball, and now she wants to play volleyball. If it has a ball, if it moves, if she has to shove aside three other players first, she'll be the first to the ball every time."

Of course, that made perfect sense.

"What did her father do? Is he athletic?" Lori asked.

Martel smiled. "Yes. You would say that."

LORI ASKED IF Martel was still teaching. They let her know that Mark had accepted the administrator's job at a large charter school in the area. Lori was now working toward her degree in counseling and administration, but teaching was still her first love.

"Where did you get the name Ainsley?" Martel asked.

"It was my mother's."

"It's beautiful."

They laid down ground rules for a meeting, giving them time to sit down with her and make sure her daughter was comfortable with it. It was decided that sometime in February when the school had a ski week break would be best, and Martel agreed.

"We talked between us about the possibility she might want to reach out to you someday." Mark frowned. "Are we still of the same opinion?" he asked his wife before he continued.

"Yes, I feel comfortable with that."

"We decided that it should be her choice, not yours and not ours," he said.

"I can honor that. I think we have to be very transparent. I don't want any secrets." Martel nearly choked on that word.

"Exactly."

Before they parted, Martel reached into her purse for the leather folder with the pictures of her pregnancy, nearly month by month.

But the package wasn't there.

CHAPTER 19

D AMON JOINED RENNY and a couple of the single Team guys at the Scupper. It didn't feel like two days before Christmas. He'd brought Martel some expensive lingerie, but now he wasn't sure she'd be around to open them up. So he didn't bother buying a Christmas tree. Kyle, Cooper, T.J., Fredo, and several other married guys with kids were busy attending ballet recitals, quick trips to Disneyland or one of the Aquariums, or a Mexican cruise.

The banter was stupid. He felt like a loser, listening to stories about trying to bag girls, as if that was everything in the whole world. Several wanted to know about Florida, especially if there was good action there. He humored them. He lied. And he felt shitty about it, too.

Taking another drag on his long-necked beer, he caught a whiff of his own body odor. He hadn't shaved nor taken a shower since he'd taken Martel to the airport yesterday.

Renny slid closer to him, and Damon frowned and slid away. "Get off me."

"What's eaten your candy cane, asshole?"

Damon shrugged.

"So who is this friend she wants to visit?"

"Beats me. Some chick she met in Oregon."

Renny considered something before he spoke. "You know, lesbian girls can be pretty hot. Have you seen—"

Damon shoved him off the bench and walked out to the strand.

Like a fly on a piece of flypaper, Renny was that stray dog that would never leave him alone. He ran, catching up to him, and just matched Damon's long strides. Even assuming the position.

"See, if you're mad, Damon, you gotta walk like this." He slapped Damon's bicep and pointed to himself. "You kinda hunker down and slink down the sidewalk." He exaggerated leaning back, letting his legs kick out in front of him like the cartoons on the old R. Crumb comics.

Damon had loved those books. The beefy girls had perfectly round tits and thighs that could crush a man's head between them. Quirky and an acquired taste, but he liked them.

Charlene made him get rid of them when they got

married. Renny had been right about her all along.

It was impossible to be mad at Renny for too long. He was an easy friend because he wasn't discerning. He'd taken that knife blade to the chest to defend the Senator's daughter and never complained about it once. Renny had expected at least a phone call from the Senator. They teased him no-end about it.

He was proud to be part of one of the most successful raids they'd done and it made up for the last two that didn't go so well. They'd rescued over forty women and six children. They were due to be shipped out to South America, headed eventually to the U.S. or Canada. From there, the women would be lost, the children used and abused or worse, snuffed out. It felt good to clean out their inventory of death and destruction.

But except for a very few, the general public would never know. The Senator was too busy running for re-election. At least that's what they told Renny. This type of operation could never be leaked.

So maybe that was weighing on his mind as well. Just a confluence of timing that wasn't working for him. Unfinished business, because the bad guys would always be out there. Some of the good guys would pay the price, have accidents. That was unfair, but what they signed on for.

He owed Renny an apology.

"Sorry, man. I'm in a lousy mood. I shouldn't have come."

"You did the right thing. You were alone and wondering what she was up to. I'd feel the same way, except I would have snuck up and had her followed. And then, if there was a woman, or another guy, I would have pounded the shit out of them, either way."

Damon knew Renny wouldn't do that.

"So what is it, really? Just spill it. I'll make it worse!" Renny said brightly.

"I don't know," he lied. He didn't tell anyone he'd asked her to marry him and she'd turned him down. *Nicely* turned him down someone would say. As if there was anything nice about it. He missed their connection, the intensity with which she gave herself to him. He wanted to inhabit every square inch of her body, her thoughts and her soul. He couldn't help it if he was selfish. He'd had a taste of that, and he got hooked forever.

'I'm done looking' he'd told her. Maybe he nixed it by not buying her a ring. But what they had was bare naked truth and that sense of belonging as if they were originally one body and somehow got separated and now found each other again. He didn't want anyone else. He didn't want to pretend to be happy. He wanted to feel like he did when they were skydiving. Watching the wonder in her face as she screamed, even if she did

slime him. He held her arms out, felt her joy and mirth melting into him as he kept her in the air, opening up her world to the view from thirteen thousand feet.

Not every man could do that for his woman. Not every woman could be present for it. It took someone special to let him be in control, to understand that he loved teaching her about flying, about sex, about what this whole brotherhood thing was all about. He thought all that was important to her, because it was important to him.

Renny had been prattling on about something he hadn't been paying attention to.

"Ice cream?"

"Sure."

They hadn't really had dinner, but he didn't want any. Renny ordered a sundae for him because he didn't care. He checked his phone and didn't get a text from her saying she was back. That either meant that she'd stayed another night, or she didn't want him to pick her up, or worse yet, she'd flown all the way back to Florida.

"Fuck it."

"Fuck what?" Renny brought his waffle cone Sundae covered in chocolate sauce and whipped cream, placing it right in front of him.

He stared at the whipped cream, let his finger dive into it and brought a huge glob to his mouth.

"I got a spoon here, Damon." Renny passed the white plastic utensil over the table for him.

"I don't want to eat it with a spoon. I want to eat it with my finger."

Renny put it down and stared at him. "Something's not right here."

He thought about it then scooped up another fingerfull and stared down the street.

The sky was orange as the sun set. There were so many things like Florida, and so many things that were completely different.

"Do you know whipped cream tastes different here?" he said to Renny.

"You guys broke up. She's not coming back. That's what happened."

"I can always tell when I'm being lied to. It's one thing to have a woman lie to you about your performance. I don't mind that kind of lie because they just want to make you feel special and all. But when they say they want to be a part of your life and then hide something really big, that kind of a lie makes me feel like I've been stupid."

"Are you sure you're not overreacting? Maybe you should talk to Kyle, or Coop or one of the other guys. Just how do you know she's not leveling with you?

"I don't know, but I just know. I'll find out, eventually. Ten years from now, I'll be at some second or third wedding for you or one of the other guys, and she'll just walk into the room. We'll stand there, sniff the air, and test our ability to make each other miserable."

"Holy shit, Damon. This scares me. That's it. I'm staying over tonight. We're going to get some movies and we're going to get you so fuckin' drunk you'll think you were back in Florida."

"You know what, Renny? Maybe I am. Maybe I am."

THEY'D STOPPED BY to buy some snacks and beers. Damon bought just about every kind of chocolate bar he could find in the liquor store. The Indian clerk squinted at him, lowering his forehead in disapproval.

"What? I have a sweet tooth," Damon said. Renny was still cruising for the perfect bag of chips.

"No man, you have a death wish. That stuff'll kill you, my man," he said in his clipped Indian accent.

"It's chocolate!"

"Yes, and a whole lot of other things too. But it's your life, my man."

Yes, it is my life. The clerk had been exactly right. This was his way of dealing because he didn't want to think too hard on two things: what he was missing, and how to fix it.

BACK AT DAMON'S place, Renny started straightening up the dishes left with cereal and milk stuck to the sides of the bowl. He picked up a pair of jeans and a shirt, moved his shoes to the side where they wouldn't trip on them, and then walked into the bedroom.

"Come on, Damon, let's wash your sheets. That will help you sleep better. That's what you need."

"I thought we were going to watch movies tonight," Damon said as he began stripping off the blanket and the top sheet then the bottom sheet.

"We will. We put these into the wash, and then we settle down and watch some serious porn. This way, when you wake up with a headache, at least your sheets will smell nice. Unlike the rest of you."

Renny was right. Damon picked up the bundle and walked to the bathroom where his stacking washer-dryer was. He stuffed the sheets and blanket into the front loader. As he swung the door closed, a leather folder, like ones that hold pictures, fell to the ground. He picked it up and sat on the bed.

They were pictures of Martel when she was much younger. The photo was taken from the side, so that in each one, her belly got bigger and bigger.

These are pictures of Martel being pregnant.

He let the photos drop to the floor as he braced his forehead in his hand.

So that's where she's gone. She's had a baby with

someone. She's gone to see her child and to be with the man who gave her that child. That's the secret she didn't want to tell him. It wasn't a woman she was visiting. It was a man.

Her lover.

Renny didn't ask anything when he saw Damon sitting on the bare mattress. Instead he knelt, picking up the photos and one by one examined them, and then put them into the leather pouch.

"I don't understand, Damon. What are these?"

"It's the reason she isn't coming back."

"But what does it mean?" Renny asked.

"What do you think it means? That's Martel, god-dammit."

"But how—?"

Just then, they heard Damon's door open. Renny stood, but Damon remained seated. Martel appeared in the entrance, righting her suitcase. She saw the folder in Renny's hands, walked over and took the package from him.

Renny looked between Martel and Damon and back again. "Sh-Sh-should I leave?"

No one said a word, so Renny slipped on his jacket, stepped into his canvas slip-ons and did just that.

Damon couldn't look at her. Once again, he felt cold. He had no way to put all this together. He wanted information but he didn't want to ask.

She walked in front of him and sat down on the bed beside him. Her pretty pink nails opened the pouch, worn and scuffed, opening the flap enclosed with a Velcro tab. She pulled out the pictures, neatly tucked into plastic sleeves, and placed the stack on her knees.

Martel put her arm around Damon's shoulder. At first he wanted to pull away, but she held him, then pressed her forehead against his, with her right hand holding the pictures in her lap. She held up one, searching his eyes for any expression.

"This picture was taken about four months after you left Santa Rosa."

She wasn't smiling.

He looked at it again, and then took it in his fingers, squinting to see it more clearly.

"This picture," she said as she held a second one up, "was taken a month later."

Damon added it to the other one.

"And this one the month after that."

He took the picture from her hand again and stacked it with the other two.

"And this one, and this one, and finally this one. I took this one when I was living up in Oregon by the ocean. I stayed there while I had the baby, Damon. Your baby. Our baby. Our little girl. And I made sure she got a chance at life. I interviewed and found the perfect parents for her. That's what I did ten years ago while you were off being a Boy Scout."

Damon's finger rubbed the last photo, tracing the outline of Martel's belly over and over again.

She leaned into him and whispered in his ear, "I found her, Damon. She's beautiful."

He searched her eyes, streaming tears. He was a jumble of emotions. Part of him was angry, part was scared, and there was a huge part that loved this woman and what she had done. She'd taken care of his little girl when he wasn't capable of being there for either one of them. He didn't deserve her. He really didn't.

"Say something, Damon."

"I'm ashamed."

She adjusted his hand so he could look at the pictures again. "No, we made a mistake. But *she* wasn't one of them."

"So this is what you were doing?"

"Yes. I haven't spoken to her yet. I met with her parents. I asked, and they agreed to meet with me. I wanted to see her, Damon, and they've agreed."

"But why? I mean, why would they let you come in and upset everything?"

"Because I'm not. She belongs to them now, not to me, or us. They are her parents and always will be. I just wanted to see her happy and tell her that I love her, that she's always been loved. Not abandoned. Loved. Wouldn't you want to know that if it was you?"

"But what about us?"

"This changes nothing, Damon. This was the one thing I needed to do, to clear up on my own. It was that hole in my soul nothing or no one in this world could fill."

She reached down into her purse and brought out the picture.

"This is Ainsley, your daughter."

His eyes filled with tears as she held him. He swallowed hard, unable to speak, overcome with the miracle presented to him. Finally, he found his courage. "Do I get to meet her?" he asked.

"If you want to. If she wants to. If we get permission. But some day, Damon, I'm sure you will. Can you be patient?"

He dropped the pictures and pulled her close to him. It all came into focus now. He'd left. He went off, running from the only miracle in his life. But Martel never did. She never left. She kept the dream and the flame alive.

As long as she was beside him, he'd let her teach him that. As long as they were together, anything was possible.

EPILOGUE

ONE OF THE first things Martel did when she returned to Florida was to visit Phyllis at the cemetery. She sat on the cold stone bench nearby, contemplating the headstone engraved with the face of an angel and Phyllis' dates. She had been buried beside her late husband.

"You're going to have to give me a sign, tell me what he thought of your red dress and your choice of reading material. I hope you didn't get into too much trouble about your evenings dancing under the stars with that handsome Jamaican fellow. Did he sing to you, I wonder?"

She could see it all clearly. Phyllis, young and healthy, smiling and showing everyone around her how fearless she was.

She listened to sounds of an ordinary day. Phyllis didn't respond.

"I found her, Phyllis. Her name is Ainsley, and

she's a doll. We're arranging a meet and greet right around Valentine's Day. Her mother says she's gifted in sports. Who knew, right?"

SHE DROVE BACK toward the coast and north, passing the ice cream shops and fish places along the two-lane highway, driving through towns so small that if she blinked, she'd miss them completely. Here it was January, and people waded around in their bathing suits and flip-flops, carrying beach chairs, dragging wheeled coolers behind them—stopping traffic— headed for the beach. There were no freeways, very few high-rises, and everyone was from someplace else.

Martel was coming full circle. She'd been drawn here by a friend on vacation. Her friend went back to California, and Martel stayed. She found her little beach bungalow, where she could wake up late at night and see the glistening waves in the moonlight. She loved the power of the orange and purple hues at Sunset—that time of day when the sky seemed to fall and cover everyone in gold.

Walking back inside her rented place, she knew she was going to miss how safe she'd felt here, how her discarded fears and new dreams adorned the walls, like a spell, keeping all the good inside and shedding off the bad.

Her journey had been rocky, but she'd managed to

finish on her feet, fate having brought the man she'd always loved back into her life. In June, she'd be moving out of this little place. Someone else would call it home, and she hoped for them it would bring all the magic and happiness she felt while living here.

She and Damon compromised on the wedding. She had people in Florida who would want to attend. He had friends in San Diego who wanted the party. So, they planned a small early June wedding and reception at the gazebo at the beach and the audience would sit facing the ocean. Martel and Damon would take their vows at sunset and watch until the sun dropped into the water.

Then they'd leave for their honeymoon in San Diego, starting with a reception for all of Damon's Team buddies and family in California, on to her new life with her SEAL husband. There was an adventure there, for sure, but she'd miss this place.

Her landlady said she hoped Martel and Damon would return and gave them two free weeks of their choosing as a wedding present. It was their first one.

It was a tradition she wanted to keep, once a year coming back to this place that meant so much to her. A place she ran to when she needed it, the place that healed her and brought her the man she loved and much more.

There was a lot to look forward to between now

and June. Top of her list was her Valentine's trip to California where she'd get to meet Ainsley for the first time. She had feelers out at several schools in the San Diego area, and she hoped to interview.

But mostly, she planned on enjoying the peace and calm, living alone, and preparing for the rest of her life. When she closed that door for the last time, she didn't want any regrets. After all, her adventure was only beginning.

And no matter where she was, her heart would always be here, on the white sugary sand and clear blue waters at Sunset Beach.

You can find that beautiful story, in Martel and Damon's story, continued, in Second Chance Reunion.

Did you enjoy Second Chance SEAL? Stay tuned for my next book, Treasure Island SEAL, where a pirate SEAL rescues his mermaid—diving deep for dangerous love, coming this summer. Watch for the announcement of the release dates.

And if Book 2 is the first book you've read in the Sunset SEALs series, then won't you try **SEALed At Sunset**, Book 1? It's available in print and audio versions as well.

If you want the whole over-arching series, beginning with my very first SEAL Brotherhood book, **Accidental SEAL**, you can get the entire first four books plus two novellas in my **Ultimate SEAL Collection No. 1**. You'll be introduced to Kyle, Coop, Fredo, Armando and others as they begin their journey together into your hearts. You can also get the bundle in **audio format** as well. This was the start of the whole series, hatched when I was bumped from a United flight home to San Francisco and stayed in a place called Lansdowne Resort. Kyle Lansdowne was created that night!

As in all my books, many of the stories are my fictional and romantic adaptations of events that actually occurred, either in my life or those I've had the pleasure to meet. Not everyone comes home from their missions in real life. I like to think I save a few of them and as long as you read, they will live forever.

ABOUT THE AUTHOR

NYT and USA/Today Bestselling Author Sharon Hamilton's SEAL Brotherhood series have earned her author rankings of #1 in Romantic Suspense, Military Romance and Contemporary Romance. Her other *Brotherhood* stand-alone series are: Bad Boys of SEAL Team 3, Band of Bachelors, True Blue SEALs, Nashville SEALs, Bone Frog Brotherhood, Sunset SEALs, Bone Frog Bachelor Series and SEAL Brotherhood Legacy Series. She is a contributing author to the very popular Shadow SEALs multi-author series.

Her SEALs and former SEALs have invested in two wineries, a lavender farm and a brewery in Sonoma County, which have become part of the new stories. They also have expanded to include Veteran-benefit projects on the Florida Gulf Coast, as well as projects in Africa and the Maldives. One of the SEAL wives has even launched her own women's fiction series. But old characters, as well as children of these SEAL heroes keep returning to all the newer books.

Sharon also writes sexy paranormals in two series: Golden Vampires of Tuscany and The Guardians.

A lifelong organic vegetable and flower gardener,

Sharon and her husband lived for fifty years in the Wine Country of Northern California, where many of her stories take place. Recently, they have moved to the beautiful Gulf Coast of Florida, with stories of shipwrecks, the white sugar-sand beaches of Sunset, Treasure Island and Indian Rocks Beaches.

She loves hearing from fans through her website: authorsharonhamilton.com

Find out more about Sharon, her upcoming releases, appearances and news when you sign up for Sharon's newsletter.

Facebook:
facebook.com/SharonHamiltonAuthor

Twitter:
twitter.com/sharonlhamilton

Pinterest:
pinterest.com/AuthorSharonH

Amazon:
amazon.com/Sharon-Hamilton/e/B004FQQMAC

BookBub:
bookbub.com/authors/sharon-hamilton

Youtube:
youtube.com/channel/UCDInkxXFpXp_4Vnq08ZxMBQ

Soundcloud:
soundcloud.com/sharon-hamilton-1

Sharon Hamilton's Rockin' Romance Readers:
facebook.com/groups/sealteamromance

Sharon Hamilton's Goodreads Group:
goodreads.com/group/show/199125-sharon-hamilton-readers-group

Visit Sharon's Online Store:
sharon-hamilton-author.myshopify.com

Join Sharon's Review Teams:

eBook Reviews:
sharonhamiltonassistant@gmail.com

Audio Reviews:
sharonhamiltonassistant@gmail.com

Life is one fool thing after another.
Love is two fool things after each other.

REVIEWS

even finished it up in a day. The vampires in this book were different from your average vampire, but I enjoy different variations and changes to the same old stuff. It made for a more unpredictable read and more adventurous to explore! Vampire lovers, any paranormal readers and even those who love the romance genre will enjoy Honeymoon Bite."

"This is the first non-Seal book of this author's I have read and I loved it. There is a cast-like hierarchy in this vampire community with humans at the very bottom and Golden vampires at the top. Lionel is a dark vampire who are servants of the Goldens. Phoebe is a Golden who has not decided if she will remain human or accept the turning to become a vampire. Either way she and Lionel can never be together since it is forbidden.

I enjoyed this story and I am looking forward to the next installment."

"A hauntingly romantic read. Old love lost and new love found. Family, heart, intrigue and vampires. Grabbed my attention and couldn't put down. Would definitely recommend."

PRAISE FOR THE
BAD BOYS OF SEAL TEAM 3 SERIES

"I love reading this series! Once you start these books, you can hardly put them down. The mix of romance and suspense keeps you turning the pages one right after another! Can't wait until the next book!" (5 Star Review)

"I love all of Sharon's Seal books, but *[SEAL's Code]* may just be her best to date. Danny and Luci's journey is filled with a wonderful insight into the Native American life. It is a love story that will fill you with warmth and contentment. You will enjoy Danny's journey to become a SEAL and his reasons for it. Good job Sharon!" (5 Star Review)

PRAISE FOR THE
BAND OF BACHELORS SERIES

"*[Lucas]* was the first book in the Band of Bachelors series and it was a phenomenal start. I loved how we got to see the other SEALs we all love and we got a look at Lucas and Marcy. They had an instant attraction, and their love was very intense. This book had it all, suspense, steamy romance, humor, everything you want in a riveting, outstanding read. I can't wait to read the next book in this series." (5 Star Review)

PRAISE FOR THE
TRUE BLUE SEALS SERIES

"Keep the tissues box nearby as you read *True Blue SEALs: Zak* by Sharon Hamilton. I imagine more than I wish to that the circumstances surrounding Zak and Amy are all too real for returning military personnel and their families. Ms. Hamilton has put us right in the middle of struggles and successes that these two high school sweethearts endure. I have read several of Sharon Hamilton's military romances but will say this is the most emotionally intense of the ones that I have read. This is a well-written, realistic story with authentic characters that will have you rooting for them and proud of those who serve to keep us safe. This is an author who writes amazing stories that you love and cry with the characters. Fans of Jessica Scott and Marliss Melton will want to add Sharon Hamilton to their list of realistic military romance writers." (5 Star Review)

"Dear FATHER IN HEAVEN,

If I may respectfully say so sometimes you are a strange God. Though you love all mankind,

It seems you have special predilections too.

You seem to love those men who can stand up alone who face impossible odds, Who challenge every bully and every tyrant ~

Those men who know the heat and loneliness of Calvary. Possibly you cherish men of this stamp because you recognize the mark of your only son in them.

Since this unique group of men known as the SEALs know Calvary and suffering, teach them now the mystery of the resurrection ~ that they are indestructible, that they will live forever because of their deep faith in you.

And when they do come to heaven, may I respectfully warn you, Dear Father, they also know how to celebrate. So please be ready for them when they insert under your pearly gates.

Bless them, their devoted Families and their Country on this glorious occasion.

We ask this through the merits of your Son, Christ Jesus the Lord, Amen."

By Reverend E.J. McMalhon S.J. LCDR, CHC, USN
Awards Ceremony SEAL Team One
1975 At NAB, Coronado

www.ingramcontent.com/pod-product-compliance
Lightning Source LLC
Chambersburg PA
CBHW060154180626
46813CB00007B/2742